WHEN GUNNAR MARTINSON'S FRANCHISE ROBOTS GO CRAZY

Crime Novel No. 2 ° English Edition

Veronika Bellone & Thomas Matla

WHEN GUNNAR MARTINSON'S FRANCHISE ROBOTS GO CRAZY

Crime Novel No. 2 ° English Edition

THE SWISS FRANCHISE DETECTIVES

WHEN GUNNAR MARTINSON'S FRANCHISE ROBOTS GO CRAZY
Book series: THE SWISS FRANCHISE DETECTIVES
Crime Novel No. 2 – English Edition
© 2024 Veronika Bellone & Thomas Matla
Kontakt@Kunstwirtschaftler.com www.Kunstwirtschaftler.com
Publisher: BoD • Books on Demand GmbH, In de Tarpen 42, 22848 Norderstedt
Printed by: Libri Plureos GmbH, Friedensallee 273, 22763 Hamburg
ISBN (Print): 978-3-7597-7509-2

Preface

In this second volume of the new franchise crime series *The Swiss Franchise Detectives* Lars Van de Velde is called to the Zug headquarters of the Happy People fitness franchise. It relies heavily on robotics and artificial intelligence, but is being blackmailed. Obviously, not all franchisees act in accordance with the system. During his investigations in Berlin and Hamburg (Germany) as well as Unterägeri and Zug (Switzerland) Lars has to experience first-hand how robots can help, but also endanger human lives.

Loretta Lombardi, not averse to all things Italian and sensual, and Lars Van de Velde, an Amsterdam born cycling and Japan enthusiast, are partners of the Swiss detective agency *Lombardi International Franchise Investigations AG*, in Zug. Both detectives fight for the good in franchising, track down black sheep and solve mysterious cases. More than once, they have to make use of their fighting skills.

When Gunnar Martinson's Franchise Robots Go Crazy

1

When Liliane woke up on that sunny spring Saturday, she knew it would be a beautiful day. Finally, after such a long time, she would meet her best girlfriends again. But she had no idea what turn the day would take and how much it would change her life forever. Now it was time for her morning toilet, although her personal time out was more reminiscent of a physical culture program. She took a lot of time for this every day. It also helped her to organize herself mentally on a daily basis. When she came out of the bathroom later, the fresh smell of coffee was already wafting through the large rooms of the apartment on Lake Zug. Reto, her husband, took advantage of the unexpected heat wave and prepared her a sumptuous breakfast on the balcony for the first time in the year. He waved to her. As she approached, she noticed the smell of the fresh baked goods. Her mouth immediately watered.

"Reto, you are such an angel and the best husband I could ever wish for!" Liliane sat down at the table and drank the freshly squeezed orange juice. She didn't lack anything. Reto had cooked fresh eggs and also thought of her favorite jam, lemon-ginger. This was accompanied by fresh croissants from the old town bakery. He was currently pouring Prosecco into heavy crystal glasses. She watched him in silence. He was slightly shorter than her, even when sitting. She saw his hair slowly thinning and his scalp increasingly shining through. Soon a shiny circle would appear that would give him something settled. Their age difference, she was ten years younger, was also reflected in his increasing waist size. Physically he became increasingly rounder, softer and more feminine. He concealed his emerging physical weaknesses through his activities, his ingenuity and his unconditional loyalty and devotion to her.

"Do you want to wrap me in a cotton-soft, permanent dream from which I never wake up?" she asked him, smiling. "First you spoil me all night long. Now this wonderful breakfast. Life can be so beautiful." She enjoyed his attention and his devotion. She admired how intensely he loved her. He would do anything for her, she knew that for sure. She, on the other hand, was infinitely grateful for it, but incapable of his love to reply. She would never be able to love him the way he loved her. She looked into the distance, lost in thought. The balcony offered a wide view over Lake Zug. It was at the back of her old town apartment, at the top of the house. She often sat here and dreamed when she was alone. Dark dreams, with dark angels passing like clouds in her mind's eye. Sometimes they stayed, even for long periods of time. Reto then tried to cheer up his wife, to encourage her, to do something good for her. But he often spent nights working in his IT office, in the Zug office center, near the train station. Liliane then stayed to herself, alone in her dark inner world. How different she had imagined her life to be before. This often gave her deep thoughts about it. So far, she has always managed to emerge from it, even if it became more difficult and took longer each time. She tried to accept what couldn't be changed, at least most of the time. The spring sun was shining and the splendor of the flowers was overwhelming. It was warm in the canton of Zug, far too warm for the time of year. That's why Liliane chose a light dress for her trip. A yellow one with small floral motifs that went well with her long, curly red hair. In the afternoon she said goodbye with a quick kiss to her husband, who had encouraged her to meet her best girlfriends. She got on her yellow Pedelec, which was parked behind the house, and cycled directly along the lakeshore to a small restaurant with a boat dock. Her girl friends were already waiting there eagerly for her. Their greetings were stormy. Liliane immediately felt years younger and more alive.

Like her girlfriends, she began to make childish jokes. Everyone was talking non-stop, mostly at the same time, eating small snacks and drinking Aperol Spritz. Liliane hadn't felt this well for a long time. She had completely forgotten and perhaps even missed these stories and conversations in recent years.

After the sudden death of her parents, she withdrew from all her friends and into her dark inner world, in which she lived for a long time. Suddenly there was bright light and sunshine, color and happiness among her friends. She didn't know if she could allow this closeness and the intense feelings again. She didn't trust them. But all the stories from her childhood and youth were probably part of her. She had completely suppressed all of it recently. She grew up in a sheltered place in the small village of Oberägeri, right next to beautiful Lake Ägeri. Her father worked for the community and was known and respected throughout the valley. He drove a yellow Citroen 2CV. A yellow that she really liked. As a child she was deeply impressed by her father. He was the authority figure for her. She tried to achieve a similar position, but in vain. At school, the boys teased her because of her red hair. She accepted this patiently, just like her red-haired mother. She loved her mother more than anyone else. She was the real center of the family. Also, the absolute master of the bakery. Little Liliane was able to use her cookies as exchange currency at school and in return she got everything a child's heart could desire, even a ride on her school friend Valentin's *Pony* moped. In her childhood days, Liliane actually learned from her mother everything she needed to influence boys, and later men. Then childhood and youth were suddenly over. Liliane moved abroad to study in Hamburg. It was difficult for her to separate from her home village. Her wishes and dreams helped her. They seemed to come true faster than expected. She fell in love, head over heels, for the first time into a fellow student. They both moved into a small apartment in the Winterhude district of Hamburg, near his parents.

At the end of their studies, they went on a trip around the world that ended in Japan. Here they got engaged under cherry blossoms. Here they also discovered a new business idea that should have meant their future. They wanted to be the first to bring it to Germany. But then everything turned out completely different. Out of nowhere, a huge argument developed between them and, unexpectedly, her fiancé broke up with her. From one day to the next, all her plans for the future were dashed. Without an explanation. She never spoke about it to anyone. Especially not with her girl-friends on such a beautiful evening on Lake Zug.

The evening had actually come much quicker than expected. The group agreed to meet up again and left the restaurant one after the other. Liliane was the last to leave, as she had invited everyone and was picking up the bill. She suddenly had to stop on the narrow path to the exit. A couple was walking towards her, hugging each other. She recognized the man immediately. A pain shot through her, like a stab in the solar plexus. As if a knife were stuck in her stomach and spun around its own axis several times. She remained rooted to the spot. Right in front of both of them. She bent slightly. Looked at him. He ignored her and seemed completely fixated on his partner. More casually, he asked her to let her walk past with a demanding gesture of his hand. Liliane saw the smile of the beautiful woman at his side. And in an instant, they were gone. She stood there for a while. Just like that. Frozen and unable to move. She couldn't turn around or move on. Her stomach ached, her temples throbbed and she felt nauseated. She also had a slight flicker in front of her eyes, as if there wasn't enough blood in her head. All her feelings were the same as when he suddenly separated from her, so long ago. Maybe even worse. Later, Liliane didn't know whether she had said goodbye to her girlfriends or how she got home. She was so happy that Reto was waiting for her there. She stopped pretending and let her feelings run wild. She poured her heart out to him and told him for the first time what she had been keeping quiet for all these years. She told him about her sudden encounter with her former fiancé in the restaurant. About the deep pain of the past that had resurfaced. Several times she switched from serious concern, to deep sadness and childlike helplessness, to open hysteria. "I could kill him!" she finally moaned, "for all the pain, suffering and wounds he has caused me." Anger and fury were written on her face. "Someone really needs to punish him! Painfully and persistently." Reto knew about her depressive falls and feared her very much. Liliane could be so euphoric, so infectiously positive and life-affirming. Then everything was possible and the sky had no limits. At her peak, she overcame seemingly insurmountable obstacles. That's how he met her. That's how he loved her. But when her depressive episodes began, there was only one direction to go, downwards. She could suddenly fall into a deep hole. Everything around her went black in fast motion. These phases came unpredictably. Just like that day. They were usually intense, long and difficult. Dullness spread throughout the apartment. Filled it with darkness. Nothing was worth anything anymore. Neither her own life, nor her relationship with Reto or with her friends. Reto suffered with her. Every time more. Over the years he couldn't find a suitable way to help her out of this fatal vicious circle and became increasingly helpless. That's why he had been using avoidance for a long time, without knowing exactly what would trigger her depression. Over the last few months, he had made every effort to make their life together and their relationship positive, joyful and lively. To this day he had been successful with it. Now, out of the blue, a black phase would set in and all his efforts would again be in vain. This time, however, there was a concrete cause of her suffering. One she had never spoken to him about before. It was probably the original source of her years of dark thoughts and the slow death in their relationship.

2

Lars Van de Velde stood at the open window and looked calmly into the dawn. He had been in Switzerland for five years now. Moved here to become a partner in the Zug detective agency *Lombardi - International Franchise Investigations AG*. A lot of things were still foreign to him. But not this view from the window. He enjoyed it every morning as much as possible. At this early hour, the *Rigi* and the *Pilatus* were only vaguely visible as mountains. *Lake Zug* lay dozing outside the window. No boat was on the way. Only the wind occasionally caused the waves to lap at the boat docks, which sounded like they were at the sea. Especially when that wind called *Bise* came along. Just a few ducks took turns chasing each other. Their loud chattering made Lars happy. He enjoyed his first green tea of the day. He liked the silence when no one was in the office yet. No excited chatter, no strange thoughts and no different opinions. The day was able to unfold, very slowly. Lars watched the waking day closely. He had also carefully selected the tea. A Hon-Yuu Sencha, from the small island of Yakushima. A first flush, from tea bushes that had grown in the open air, without any shade from trees. The tea ceremony was his morning ritual, his Zen. With it he gathered and centered himself and awakened his body, his mind and his soul. Lars loved this gentle awakening and the clarity that followed.

He inherited the Japanese philosophy of life from his parents, more precisely from his mother. She was born as Himari Kobayashi in Kyoto, Japan, and met Daan Van de Velde at a bicycle trade fair in Tokyo when she was 21. Lars' father Daan was a Dutch native from Amsterdam and the third-generation owner of a bicycle factory. It was love at first sight when he met Himari, whose name in German translation was Sunshine. It described her very appropriately. Six months later they both got married in Amsterdam because Lars had announced his arrival. His brother Finn followed two years later. Lars, with his adult height of one meter eighty, a rather stocky build, blue eyes and dark blonde short hair, was supposed to take after his father and looked very Dutch. His mother's Japanese moved inward. It showed in the way he thought and acted as well as in his preferences, values and his special way of living. He also acquired Japanese language skills as a child.

The loud office telephone suddenly tore Lars out of his thoughts. A Zug phone number appeared on the display.

"Lombardi International Franchise Investigations, Van de Velde on the line." A male voice answered, trying to speak standard German, but with a slightly Nordic accent.

"Good morning Mr. Van de Velde. This is Gunnar Martinson, from the Happy People. We are an internationally active fitness and wellness company. I am the founder and managing director. I'm glad you're here so early. Do you have a moment?"

"Yes, how can I help you?"

"I came across your detective agency because we are expanding via franchising. Mr. Van de Velde, we have an urgent problem. I would therefore like to speak to you at short notice. Direct, personal and confidential. We are also in Zug. Could you possibly come to our headquarters? Today? Maybe right now? I know it sounds unusual, but if you could somehow make it happen..."

"I have an appointment at 11 a.m. You are located on the Siemens site, right?" Lars had switched on his laptop and was scrolling down the Happy People website. "I could be with you by 8 o'clock."

"Thanks! That's wonderful." Lars was quickly persuaded that day. At the moment he was happy with any customer meeting, no matter how short notice it took place. He longed to be on the road with his bike. It was spring. The sun was already invigoratingly bright, the air was so smooth, the wind was so refreshing. He felt the longed-for spring energy. He would have liked to do nothing but cycle. Through all of Switzerland. He would also like to go further, to the south of France, Italy or Spain, where the battery and his muscle power would take him. So now, to the headquarters of the Happy People. 10 minutes later he stopped in front of one of the glass towers in the Zug office center and parked his green Pedelec at a Happy People charging station, right next to the entrance. Maybe this would at least allow him to avoid the obligatory Monday meeting in the detective agency's office today. This wouldn't start until 11 a.m. and he would definitely be back by then. A little distance from the Monday meetings would be just fine with him right now. Regula, the dedicated office manager, was very warm and understanding, but Lars still couldn't really get used to the strict Swiss regulations and agenda lists.

3

A Swiss woman of about 25 years of age with subtle make-up was waiting for Lars at the Happy People reception. He could read Brigitte on her name tag.

"Hello, you must be Lars Van de Velde. Mr. Martinson is already waiting for you. I'll accompany you upstairs." Her deep blue business outfit reminded Lars a little of a German airline, her dark, velvety voice of the announcements in the arrivals hall at the international airport in Rio de Janeiro, Brazil. Except that Brigitte spoke with a Swiss-German accent. His body reacted with goosebumps. He hoped she didn't notice. She called a colleague from an adjacent room to replace her at the reception and told Lars that she would now lead him to a small cinema room on the first floor. He followed her willingly, as he would have followed her immediately and without complaint to any place in the world. Her body was well proportioned and she moved extremely smoothly. He just couldn't take his eyes off her waist. In Holland he would probably have called her *Lekker Meid.* But he wasn't sure about that anymore. This Swiss German had actually managed to completely mess up his Dutch mother tongue, or rather father tongue, in just a few years. Often, he couldn't even think of the simplest words. In addition, he was no longer sure whether such terms were even allowed to be thought and spoken anymore. Too much had changed in the last few years. He followed her up the stairs, wishing he could do this more often, including to other, more personal places.

Gunnar Martinson was fiddling with a computer when he entered the screening room. He greeted Lars from a distance and pointed to a seating area. Lars took a seat and nestled himself into the thick, soft, olive-colored leather of the Scandinavian seating. He liked green, as well as Nordic design and high-quality craftsmanship. He was immediately captivated by the Happy People's features. He felt at home. Everything was characterized by a subtle desire to create, solid quality and connoisseurship. Unfortunately, the receptionist with the goosebumps voice disappeared again. Now Gunnar Martinson turned to him. He had obviously been able to successfully complete his work on the computer.

"Mr. Van de Velde, thank you for coming so quickly. It's really serious!" Martinson seemed agitated internally, even though he tried to appear calm on the outside.

"We're being blackmailed", he sat down opposite Lars, "and I fear the worst." Gunnar Martinson was much smaller than Lars had imagined based on the volume of his voice on the phone. He must have been around 40 years old. A thick gold ring shimmered dully on his left hand. He was dressed modestly but fashionably. Dark blue suit, light blue shirt, no tie, expensive leather-soled, handmade brown shoes, no socks. He wore an expensive Swiss watch from the Jura on his wrist. His face was clean-shaven. He smelled pleasant, as if he was using an after shave with a metallic note. The short-cropped, brown, full hair looked very well-groomed.

Lars immediately stored a profile description of Gunnar Martinson in his mental memory system. His memory was full of such descriptions and functioned like one big hypertext in which everything was connected to everything else.

"What exactly happened, Mr. Martinson?" Apparently trying to calm himself, Martinson took three times a deep breath.

"I got a phone call at home. Last Saturday. A blackmailer demanded 250,000 Swiss francs." Lars pulled out his notebook, wanted to know more from Martinson and listened intently.

"When exactly did the call come and what did the voice sound like? Was it from a man or a woman?" Martinson shifted slightly on the chair.

"It was about 9:45 p.m., just before the evening news, and it was a man's voice. No voice I remember. He sounded like a native Swiss to me. The blackmailer said that if I didn't comply with his demands, very personal and compromising information would be published." Lars thought for a moment.

"What exactly was his choice of words and can you imagine what he might have meant by that?" Martinson stared into space.

"I don't remember the exact wording. But he spoke very urgently, very committedly and somehow also angrily. I don't know what the compromising thing was supposed to be. I have no idea about that."

"How should you pay the claims?" Lars continued to ask.

"We didn't get that far. I've already laughed out loud and told the blackmailer that he couldn't expect to ever get anything from us. Then I just hung up. But that probably wasn't a good strategy. Of course that didn't end the matter. The phone rang again immediately and the blackmailer was on it again. In a much louder voice, he now demanded 500,000 Swiss francs. He also threatened that I shouldn't play games with him. Mr. Van de Velde, we cannot and must not afford any scandals at the moment. We have a new investor on board and want to expand significantly. We need calm in the system and no headlines in the press.

"What are you worried about now, Mr. Martinson, and how can we help you?" Martinson looked at Lars for a long time.

"I don't know for sure either. I've never been in a situation like this before. I would like to instruct you to find the blackmailer and hand him over to the police. I would like to introduce you to our company so that you understand how important it is for us to be able to continue to grow in peace. The film lasts about 45 minutes."

"OK, that fits well. Then please get started." Lars leaned back deeper into the leather cushions.

"May I perhaps offer you something about this? Coffee, tea, water and some cookies?" asked Martinson.

"A green tea, please," Lars replied. A short time later another employee appeared and served the tea with a few cookies. She was introduced to Lars as Katharina, Gunnar Martinson's assistant. Lars looked at the tea set, a white porcelain bowl with an elaborately sewn green tea bag. The tea in it had a slight smell of algae and looked high quality. According to the logo, it seemed to come from a French dealer in Paris. Next to it stood a white drinking bowl made of the same wafer-thin porcelain and a white water jug. Surprisingly, Lars registered the small hourglass so that he could individually determine the brewing time. Martinson darkened the projection room and started an original Japanese film, with English subtitles.

"We work with the Japanese research laboratory *Human Zero*, based in Tokyo. The film shows the current state of research and development in the areas of robotics and artificial intelligence. The latest robot models are *humanoids* that can no longer be distinguished from real people. They belong to different ethnicities, can speak all world languages as native speakers using special modules and can easily fit into different cultural contexts. In addition, their AI makes them capable of learning extremely fast." One could see how fascinated and proud Martinson presented the film. He continued:

"The hardware and software, their external appearance, their hair, eyes, noses, mouths and ears, the skin texture and color, as well as their entire appearance, movement and behavior, can be configured modularly."

"Language technology has truly made huge leaps in innovation", Lars exclaimed, "all robots speak so humanly. You even notice small imperfections, like normal people in real life."

Martinson nodded in confirmation.

"One and the same model can speak standard German, but also different regional dialects. Imagine Bavarian in Munich, Saxon in Dresden, Frisian in the Cloppenburg district and Berlinish in Berlin and Brandenburg. At the same time, it can speak authentic Zurich German, Basel German and Bern German. This increases regional acceptance enormously. In addition, we can add the experiences that different age groups have had in their lives in a modular way. We can use the patterns of how they responded to challenges as generational imprints. This allows us to resonate precisely with our customer groups of different ages."

"The age of the standard robot is definitely over," stated Lars.

"Correctly. Even exotic languages, from small islands in the Pacific or from villages in the rainforest", Martinson continued, "can be booked additionally at a small cost."

Lars was deeply impressed and at the same time surprised that Martinson had already dimmed the lights again. 45 minutes flew by.

"What do you think of that, Mr. Van de Velde?" Lars sipped his tea bowl.

"I didn't know that technology had already advanced so much. The robots that I know from Zurich or Basel are mainly used in the kitchen and in the service of franchise restaurants. Most of them still look and speak very much like machines. Have you already clarified whether your customers in the fitness clubs even accept robots." Martinson smiled victoriously:

"Our customers feel more comfortable with us. Everything goes faster, more precise and safer, which is also due to our facial recognition system. By being addressed personally, our customers are more likely to gain trust, join the clubs more quickly and remain members longer. Customer loyalty increases significantly and the increase in sales is enormous." A broad smile spread across Martinson's face.

"Robots deliver consistently high quality, 24 hours a day, seven days a week and 365 days a year. They always comply with all franchise standards and process steps and are clinically clean. They do not breathe or cough, so they do not emit aerosols. Viruses don't stand a chance with us. Another plus point is their artificial intelligence. They constantly learn something new and are therefore future-compatible! With them we can multiply our services again and again without loss. *We have thus solved one of the main problems of franchising in the marketing of services.* At Happy People we have been successfully using robots for many years. At the beginning of the corona pandemic, we completely replaced all of our trainers with robots. Our experiences with this have been consistently positive!" A little irritated, Lars put his tea bowl back on the table.

"All your trainers are already robots? And your customers accept that? I mean, being trained by machines?" Martinson smiled.

"You should sign up for a trial lesson as soon as possible. I believe you too will immediately become a member and become a happier person. We offer individualized training, but also a wide range of health and wellness services, such as health checks, nutritional advice, resilience training, immunizations and massages. We were also able to choose whether to assign a gender to our robots. Our market researchers advised us to use gender-fluid robots. That would fit the times and we could easily address sub-target groups and retain them in the long term. However, we have decided to only hire and use female trainers. After all, most people are still born to mothers." Martinson laughed slightly to himself and continued.

"In our experience, they also have a universal acceptance. And what's more, we get them 10 percent cheaper. We had already had good experiences with humanoids in one of our previous pilot operations. We were still using them back then from another manufacturer. But the robot women were pretty simple." Martinson unlocked his tablet and showed Lars a few charts with illustrations, technical data and purchase prices.

"Our premium training robots from the Japanese manufacturer Human Zero are among the best humanoids available worldwide. We are the master licensee for Western Europe and have sole marketing rights for the next five years. This will secure us a place at the top." beamed Martinson.

"The sensors, haptics and language software are simply fantastic and unique in the world. We are dealing here with lifelike humanoids who will ensure an important leap forward for us."

Martinson spoke enthusiastically about his company. He was just about to present more charts with Happy People's current corporate development when Katharina, the assistant, knocked on the door and entered. She handed Martinson a writing case. As she waited patiently next to him, she smiled at Lars. Her velvety voice was similar to that of the receptionist. Lars got goosebumps again, a tingling sensation in his solar plexus, which made him somewhat uncomfortable.

"Oh yes, I forgot again, thank you, dear Katharina," said Martinson, smiling familiarly at his assistant. Turning to Lars, he continued

"... yes, maybe you should sign the contract and our *Non-Disclosure Agreement* straight away. This is our confidentiality agreement, so that everything we discuss here stays between us. Martinson gave Lars the contract with the relevant attachments, including a duplicate.

Lars scanned both of them and wordlessly noted the contract period of six months over which the investigative work was allowed to last. The fee was calculated on an hourly basis, plus expenses that really seemed more than appropriate. Plus, a hefty success bonus - the shorter the time, the higher the bonus would be! He signed both copies without saying a word, only to immediately push the contract back again.

"Katharina, can you please keep this in your files? And a copy for Mr. Van de Velde, please. I don't want to be disturbed again for the next hour." The assistant nodded at Martinson with a smile and left the room. However, before Martinson could begin another monologue, Lars stood up. "Unfortunately, I have to leave now. Please send us your charts of the company's figures as well as goals and developments so that we can take a look at them. Then we would need the contact details for your franchisees in Switzerland, Austria and Germany. And maybe you can also send us the Human Zero's Japanese information film or a link for us to view. Please send everything to our office email address so that my assistant can take care of it when I'm out of the office." Lars looked Martinson straight in the eye. "If the blackmailer contacts you again, please call me or send me an email. I have to go back to the detective agency now because I have a lot to organize." Martinson had also stood up. "Thank you again for coming so quickly. We need to locate and arrest this madman as quickly as possible. We owe that to our new investor." Martinson held out his hand to Lars and said goodbye. Katharina appeared, as if invisibly summoned, handed Lars a copy of the contract and escorted him back to reception. While Lars was walking to his Pedelec, a thought came to his mind. Something was wrong with Gunnar Martinson. He was hiding something from him. The signals from his internal warning system were unmistakable. He should find out what it was. It would perhaps help to better understand the blackmailer's motive and solve the case more quickly. There was a lot to do, but at least the fee would be right this time, Lars thought. He got on his Pedelec and cycled towards the train station and the Metalli shopping center.

4

There were still a good 30 minutes until the Monday meeting in the detective agency. That's why Lars headed for his favorite tea room. It was on Baarerstrasse, at the transition to the main train station. It was managed by a young Japanese couple from Kyoto who had only been living in Zug for a few years. Lars felt at home here, it must be due to his genes on his mother's side. He ordered matcha tea and something sweet, *daifuku* made from *mochi* and *anko*. The meeting with Gunnar Martinson flashed through his mind. He would soon report on the new franchise case at the detective agency and was looking forward to the new experiences in the field of robotics, even if he had not yet been able to explain the case. "What was it all about?" There was an anonymous blackmailer who appeared to be in possession of something compromising. What it could be was not known.

"Unusual," thought Lars.

"Who would want to blackmail a franchisor of a technology-driven fitness franchise system? Why and how could he be blackmailed?" Lars broke away from his thoughts, took an enjoyable sip of his tea and turned to his mochi. He liked that sticky rice cake. It was special because it was filled with vanilla ice cream on the inside. His attempts to recreate it at home have so far failed. While chewing, he listened to the music of a young girl band that was currently being celebrated in Japan and was playing on the Japanese streaming channel. He pulled out the small sketchpad he always had with him and made a few manga sketches of Gunnar Martinson, his assistant Katharina and Brigitte, the woman at reception. His tablemates finished their game of *Go*. The large board was full of black and white stones. The players bowed to each other. Lars knew the Go master, Tori Okiri. He envied his consistent way of life. He would also have liked to devote more time to the game, which promoted clarity and focus of thinking. Tori Okiri seemed to notice his inner unrest. He turned to Lars and spoke to him in Japanese.

"Hello Lars, it's good to always take the time to play a game." Lars nodded in agreement.

"Dear Tori, that's true, and yet sometimes there are forces that prevent you from doing so." There was a short pause before Lars continued.

"Now, for example, I have to go to the office urgently." Tori Okiri looked at him with a smile.

"There's always time, you just have to take it. How about next week?" Lars thought about it. Tori Okiri was important to him. He would allow time for a game night, because that's what it was going to be.

"At the moment I still have to drive away a few evil spirits, but we will meet shortly afterwards. Is it good? I'll get back to you. Promise!" The Go master's face brightened briefly, but then became serious. "Can I give you a little advice? You only see what you expect." Tori Okiri nodded briefly to Lars and turned back to his Go player.

"Can I get you something else, Lars?" The young owner of the tea room had come to his table and also spoke to him in Japanese. Lars was always happy to hear her Kyoto accent in her words. She looked at him intently with her black eyes.

"No, thank you very much, Koko", Lars replied as he paid the bill. "Here, that's right, the rest is for *Yōkai*, the house spirit." Koko bowed several times. After Lars had paid, he set off into Zug's old town on his Pedelec, which he affectionately called his *Green Arrow*. At the Fisheries Museum he turned right and stopped on the lake side, at his Pedelec parking lot in front of the detective agency.

5

"Good morning, Lars, it's nice that you're taking part in our meeting today." said Regula Rhyser, the office manager of the Lombardi International Franchise Investigations detective agency, greeting him. All eyes turned to him. Carmen Cadruvi, the assistant to the former sole owner and current business partner of Lars, Loretta Lombardi, was also present, as was Morita Miramoto, Lars' Japanese assistant, and Sara Antić, the telephone operator and new force in the administration. Loretta herself was missing.

"Sorry, I thought the meeting was at 11 a.m." It quickly became clear that Lars had screwed up again, because the appointment had been brought forward to 10 a.m. for today only. Regula had a private appointment and had to leave early. Somehow, deep down, he had suspected it. He would probably need some more time to really settle in here. He briefly informed Regula and the team about the new blackmail case involving the Happy People fitness franchise system and pointed out the highest level of confidentiality. Then he retreated to his office with Morita.

"Have I missed a lot, Morita-San?" asked Lars, who basically only spoke standard German or English with his assistant, while Morita answered in Swiss German. Only in emergencies did they both use Japanese, as a secret language so to speak, to prevent their conversations from being overheard.

"Not really", smiled Morita, "and Regula is actually always really nice!"

"Certainly. But what's new and why isn't Loretta there?" Lars wanted to know.

"Loretta took the train to Milan at the weekend to meet with a customer. You know her, she's going to stay there for a few days and visit her relatives and friends. By the way, on Friday I was at the headquarters of Big Tom, the bicycle franchise in Basel. The owner is really very sympathetic and a real president, you weren't exaggerating. He follows our recommendation and now wants to install the surveillance cameras in hidden places to catch the thieves if they try again. He keeps us informed."

"Thanks, Morita, that's the right keyword. As I just explained in the meeting, our new customer Happy People is now our top priority. You do the research, like always."

"Do real robots really work there as trainers?" Morita wanted to know. Lars nodded.

"Awesome!" Morita exclaimed enthusiastically.

"Please try to find out everything you can about the fitness system. You will receive further information from the franchisor Gunnar Martinson on our office email that we can evaluate. It's a strange case. The motive for the blackmail is still completely unclear."
Morita interrupted:

"I just saw that an email with several files has already been received from Gunnar Martinson. You should have received a copy of it too." They both turned to their computers. In his email, Martinson thanked him for the quick meeting and expressed his suspicion that someone close to him could be behind the blackmail. His immediate vicinity included his franchisees. He would be in constant contact with them and would meet in person several times a year. There are more opportunities and reasons than enough. In his opinion, the two franchisees from Hamburg and Berlin in particular behave strangely.

"Attached is an Excel spreadsheet with all contact details." added Morita.

"Please see if there are any abnormalities." Lars remarked and continued:

"Who is doing well and who is having problems? Who is particularly under economic pressure? Who is being talked about? Who appears in the trade press or in the tabloid press? Who uses social media and how? Maybe you'll find something about gambling addictions, big cars or unusual women? The whole sex-drugs-and-rock'n'roll program. After all, you are our deep research expert!"

"Okay, boss!" Morita agreed with a broad grin.

"But what about the criminal environment? I mean, Berlin and Hamburg, they are big cities! There are more people with criminal motives."

"I think, Morita, we can rule out contacts with real criminal circles for now. The blackmailer acts too amateurishly for that. It looks like an impulsive first act by a lone perpetrator. Maybe emotionally motivated and controlled. There should have been something that touched him deeply and encouraged him to take this step.

"So go back to *Maslow* and look for the right motive?" asked Morita.

"Yes, exactly, anything you find out can be useful. It definitely has to be quick! The faster we solve the case the higher our fee! In the meantime, I will familiarize myself with human-machine relationships, the topics of robotics and artificial intelligence, and also take a closer look at Happy People's business figures. Can you please arrange a training appointment for me at the Happy People studio in Unterägeri? Tomorrow morning, at 8 a.m. if possible. And completely privately, not as an investigator. I need to know how such robot training works.”

“It will be done, boss! I’m excited to hear what you have to say afterwards.”

“I definitely need to gain experience with this system myself. Additionally, I will try to see if I can get information from the leading robotics laboratory in Lugano, Ticino. Please keep in constant contact and keep me updated, okay?” Morita replied with his favorite phrase:

“Yes, sir!”, bowed slightly and turned back to his computer.

6

The next morning Lars stayed in bed for a short time after he woke up, which was unusual for him. There wasn't a training session with the Happy People before 9 a.m. The studio was just a few minutes by bike from his apartment. It was on Zugerstrasse, at the exit of the town. So, it made no sense to cycle down to the office in Zug and then back up again later. He surprisingly had time. He sat down at his table overlooking the Lake Ägeri and started making a few manga drawings. Strange mangas about training robots. Would they have any similarities to the real trainers? He stared at the lake, lost in thought. It was still too cold for him to swim in the lake, as the hard-core locals did before the lido officially opened. For him, things usually didn't really start until June. When he cycled to the office afterwards, he had completed a little triathlon.

His appointment today forced itself back into his consciousness. He had no idea what to expect. He felt a bit scary since he had never had direct contact before to a robot. Especially not to a female one. Now he would have to meet and talk to a robot woman. He had to spend time with her, let her guide him and maybe let her touch him. "How do you actually talk to a robot?"

he thought. "In command form, like with Internet service? Service, turn on the ambient light; Service, play Ghost Town, by the Rolling Stones; Service, put me through Loretta!" Probably not.

If the robots were really used as trainers, they would have to be able to enter into a real dialogue with customers. They would have to be able to ask questions and interpret answers. Lars still couldn't imagine how that would work.

When you saw a movie, everything was always very simple. Everything worked without you having to think about it. When watching films, people were much more tolerant and more willing to open up. The imagination did the rest. It bridged all the gaps between the artificial world and the reality. It beautified and covered up reality.

In the real world, however, Lars didn't like talking to machines. He refused to buy train tickets at the train stations from vending machines. The same at the airports. Even in the robot restaurants, he always ordered using his cell phone and avoided contact with the service robots. He would also not like to subordinate himself to a machine.

"Would the training robot woman give him instructions?" He had to stop imagining it. It would work best if he just accepted the situation. He got up and made some genmaicha tea and ate some Japanese cookies with it. Shortly before nine o'clock he got on his Green Arrow and cycled to the Happy People studio.

7

"Hello Lars. My name is Isabelle. I'm your personal trainer." "Oha!" Lars exclaimed. He hadn't expected that. Isabelle looked damn good. She was clearly not a robot, but a highly attractive young woman. Then, after the training, he had to contact the franchisee and ask why the business concept had been deviated from. Now he had to concentrate because she was just his type. "Can I offer you something? Isotonic, organic, vegan?" she asked in a velvety voice, looking him in the eyes in such a way that he got goosebumps and a tingling sensation in his stomach. That tingle in the belly again, he thought. Maybe signing up for a trial lesson as an undercover cop wasn't such a good idea after all. Lars was really no longer sure how to assess and judge the situation. Would today's appointment, although pleasant, be useless and a waste of time for his research? Should he have registered openly with the franchisee straight away? His brain was working at full speed. Could it really be that in front of him stood an astonishing specimen of the latest generation of humanoids from the Japanese technology lab Human Zero? Was he now allowed to experience it directly in action? That would be sensational, he thought. His thoughts were racing. Isabelle had stereotypical ideal dimensions, was extremely attractive and could undoubtedly make him emotional. That suggested she wasn't a machine. The way she moved, the way she spoke to him personally and looked deep into his eyes, was incredibly direct, genuine and sexy. The way few women had ever looked at him before. He knew exactly what would generally happen after that. Her voice also had this complex coloring of contradictory values. He liked the velvety and warm quality of it as well as the rough and dirty quality that sounded as if she had already looked into the depths of many human souls. He wondered how much the online survey he had to answer yesterday had influenced Isabelle's appearance and demeanor. But he immediately dismissed the idea. Such a complex creature could not be derived from the few and simple questions. Finally, his inner recognition and memorization system reported with a clear finding. Both of her wrists had a peculiarity pointing inwards. There were two small spots, not tattoos, but small pads. Because of her constant movements and the silky material, you couldn't immediately recognize it. Surfaces to navigate, like on his laptop. The red lettering on it read *Emergency Switch*. Bingo, unbelievable but true, a fembot from Human Zero. Lars took a deep breath and looked at Isabelle directly into her camera eyes, curious, fascinated and appreciative at the same time. She smiled back in confirmation. As if she could read and understand his thoughts. "Would you like something to drink now?" she asked him again. "Thank you, Isabelle, very much. Do you have any mate tea?" Now Lars was fully involved again and was looking forward to testing the android's programs in reality. "Yes, of course. I'd like to bring you a glass," she said and disappeared.

"The sales and communication software is great," thought Lars. Isabelle appeared back and handed him a chilled glass. "This is the best cold brew mate tea you can get in the entire canton of Zug."

"Thank you very much," Lars said spontaneously. He took a sip and had to nod approvingly. "It tastes extraordinary, really. But tell me, what's my training program like today?"

"I would first ask you to go to our Cabin One, take off your clothes and lie on your stomach on the lounger. We start our certified trial training with a 10-minute relaxing massage. Today it's free. As a member, you can add it to the training module as needed. This is followed by the actual 20-minute EMS training. Since both build on each other, you should always book both in the future. At the end there are still 10 minutes for nutritional advice and a personal feedback session. You can also optionally add this later as an extra module. Including changing clothes, your program lasts 45 to 50 minutes." Without waiting for a reaction from Lars, she ran ahead and opened a door for him. Her olive-colored silk suit fluttered seductively. Lars entered a small but pleasant room. Behind him she closed the door from the outside. The space was circular and seemed to be magically closed off from the outside world. There was an olive-colored lounger in the middle. The light was dimmed, only warm tones could be seen and the temperature was pleasant. There was a comfortable vanilla scent in the air. Classical music could be heard softly from somewhere. Lars recognized George Frideric Handel's fireworks music. The perfect choice of music for him. He slowly began to undress himself. With each piece of clothing, his willingness to research decreased. Finally, he lay down on his stomach on the comfortable lounger, wearing only a pair of boxer shorts. Through an opening in the headboard, he looked at the anthracite-colored linoleum floor, which slowly blurred before his eyes and became a kind of outer space. He was about to travel between two worlds. He left the cold, real world, in which everything had to be analyzed, evaluated and interpreted, and went into the sensual and emotional world, in which he could devote himself fully to the beautiful, warm and true. Later he didn't know how long he had been lying there. Nor whether he had immediately fallen into a deep sleep. Now he felt Isabelle's surprisingly delicate hands on his back. This wasn't cold, bare steel. These were sensual, warm, human hands that worked specifically on his skin and muscles. Starting at his shoulders, they gradually spread the warm oil over his entire body. He felt a pleasant warmth and enjoyed the woody scent of the oil. In the background *Handel* now started the water music. Isabelle's hands could also grip firmly. They knew the human body and all the relevant points to relax it. Lars allowed it and drifted out into the vast ocean of thoughtlessness.

"Hello Lars," he heard a whisper in his left ear. "It is time. We have already gone beyond the scope of the massage. We still want to do the exercises." He carefully opened his eyes and looked directly into Isabelle's. She returned his surprise with a smile. A shock ran through him. He had completely disappeared. Time had fully slipped away from him. He felt as if he had spent years in a deep sleep in a cozy cave in the ground and had now been kissed awake. "Yeah, sure, that's why I'm here," he said reflexively. He wanted to jump up. "Slowly, Lars. Take your time. We can go a bit overtime during the trial training. It doesn't matter and it's free today. Please use our sportswear here. I'll pick you up soon," she said and disappeared. 30 minutes later, Lars felt absolutely alive, full of energy and 10 years younger. The exercises were surprisingly a lot of fun and Isabelle knew how to motivate him and put him in an increasingly better mood. Her slightly flirty undertone did the rest. After Isabelle introduced him to delicious recipes that he could use to boost his energy levels beyond training, he was pretty happy. He said goodbye to her with a promise to try out her recipes at short notice and to coordinate the new training dates with his calendar.

"Somehow in this short time she had already become something of a good friend", thought Lars. "That something like this was possible so quickly. Maybe humanoids are better than their reputation!"

8

Lars took his green Pedelec and was about to make his way from the gym to the detective agency when he saw the missed call on his cell phone. Martinson had tried to reach him and left him a message.

"Hello Mr. Van de Velde. Things are slowly becoming dangerous. The blackmailer gave a taste of his skills and switched off all the robots for an hour in our flagship studio, here at headquarters. Our IT expert has been on it the whole time, but can't find any manipulation. At the same time, I received a text message on my cell phone with a bank account number in the British Cayman Islands. He gave me 10 days to make the transfer. Please call me back as soon as possible. Until then, greetings Martinson." Lars dialed the callback number. Martinson was on the phone immediately.

"Thank you, Mr. Van de Velde, for calling back. It must be an insider, this blackmailer. He switched off all of our training robots at headquarters. This has never happened before. My expert here is on it, but he still hasn't found anything." Lars noticed Martinson's slightly stressed voice, which no longer sounded quite as confident as it had at the beginning.

"Mr. Martinson, stay strong and don't transfer money to the blackmailer. We're in the middle of work and will try to find him." Lars heard Martinson take several breaths.

"Yes, of course, Mr. Van de Velde. I just wanted to let you know too. I'll get in touch if there's anything new." And he hung up. Lars drove down to Zug. Shortly before his arrival, as he was about to turn right in Zug's old town towards the Fisheries Museum, a red-haired woman in a yellow dress came towards him on a yellow Pedelec. It was the same brand as his. He recognized it immediately. She noticed it too. They both stopped and looked at each other.

"The advertising doesn't lie!" Lars exclaimed. "A beautiful woman on a noble bike!" She smiled. Her green eyes focused on him intently.

"And great looking men too!" she replied quickly.

"You work here, don't you! I've seen you several times from our balcony. We live above the restaurant, at the top. I'm Liliane and we are basically neighbors. We can also be on first name terms. By the way, you can eat very well here."

That was some speed, thought Lars. Completely untypical for a Swiss woman.

"Nice to meet you. I'm Lars. Yes, I work here in the detective agency. May I give you my business card?" She nodded, took it and studied it carefully.

"Aha, a detective, how exciting!" Then she put it in her fanny pack, looked around for a patio table, pointed to one and asked:

"Shall we sit down for a coffee?" I still have some time before my appointment at the hairdresser." Lars hesitated briefly.

"Well, I'm more of a tea person, but they have good tea here too." And time seemed to have sped up again, because when they got up from the table and hugged three times goodbye, it had already been a good half hour past. Lars took his Pedelec and pushed it the few meters to his parking space in front of the office.

"An attractive woman, this Liliane", he thought. She looked great, like a real model from the Swiss Pedelec brand, and appeared also clever and entertaining. And, she flirted with him. But she also seemed to have a hidden side. He noticed something deep, dark and heavy about her that didn't fit with her appearance and behavior. He knew he'd better stay away from her! In addition, he was no longer allowed to waste time pointlessly, but should concentrate fully on the research.

9

"Hoi Lars, did you have a good training session?" Morita followed Lars expectantly and curiously as he entered the detective agency and ran into the kitchen.

"Very good, Morita, I will tell you about it. Please let's get together for a status meeting right away." Lars filled all sorts of ingredients into a small bowl.

"En Guete zäme!" With a smile, Loretta joined them in the kitchen.

"Well, Lars, are you preparing your Swiss brain food again?" Lars, holding his Bircher muesli in his left hand, turned towards Loretta and greeted her.

"Yes, how lucky that Oskar invented it." They both laughed.

"It's nice to see you again, Loretta. How was Milan?"

Loretta beamed. "La Dolce Vita, how can it be otherwise? Good food, dear friends, a little bit of family and I also brought a few fashion items with me. But tell me, you have a new case?"

"Yes, it's about blackmail. But everything is still very confused. I hope we quickly see things clearly, because the faster we work, the higher is our bonus." Lars said briefly.

"Well then, get to work," said Loretta and added:

"If it's not the gardener, then it's usually a jealous wife." Lars went into his office and immediately turned to Morita:

"You can't even imagine that." He poured himself his Sencha tea.

"I was very nervous and skeptical before training. When the trainer appeared, at first, I didn't want to believe that she was a robot. She looked so real. And attractive. You hardly notice any difference to a human. If so, then in a positive way, meaning that she is better at everything. I will train there regularly. Isabelle is so motivating and uncomplicated, yet so open and honest. What you see is what you get. I think it could be a new friend. An uncomplicated robot girlfriend. That might sound strange, but I really like her a lot." Morita laughed.

"Then just be careful that Cupid doesn't catch you with his arrows!" Lars smiled and took out his cell phone. He called his combox and played the call from Martinson loudly.

"The blackmailer actually sticks around and proves his skill", commented Morita and continued, "If the IT experts of the Happy people haven't been able to find any traces so far, maybe I should go there so I can keep an eye on them."

Lars nodded. "Have you been able to find out anything yet?"

"It hasn't been very productive so far. There is nothing negative about the two franchisees, in Berlin and Hamburg. Both act in an exemplary manner and their franchise businesses run like clockwork. They are also not noticed on social media and there are no reports about them. They don't even seem to be doing any PR for themselves." Morita put on his special face again, which he always brought out when there was something strange to report.

"But what's funny is what's happening in Berlin and Hamburg outside of the ideal franchise world. In the erotic milieu there were obviously female love playmates in action. So far, they have been accused of two deaths in Hamburg and one in Berlin. This has nothing to do with the franchisees, but it is somehow interesting. The police would investigate in both cities, but until today, according to online reports, they have not found any DNA or other usable traces."

Morita added, more to himself than to Lars:

"No DNA in the redlight district, ha ha, that's impossible." Because time permitted, Morita had researched the victims' social media profiles. Coincidence or not, all three of those affected trained with the Happy People. They even posted photos of themselves with their female training robot on Instagram. It would therefore be advisable to actually visit the clubs and possibly carry out surveys. Maybe there would be a connection after all." While Morita talked, Lars entered keywords into his search engine. An article from a Hamburg newspaper appeared with the headline:

"Murder in the entertainment district. No traces whatsoever. Police are completely in the dark." The article was about a dead man on Hamburg's notorious Herbertstreet who apparently died because of his own erotic insatiability. No further details were described.

"That's bizarre, even if it has nothing to do with the case. But if both victims were really members of the Happy People, I should go to Hamburg", Lars said.

"If I leave tomorrow morning, I could be back here on Thursday, if everything goes well. Please notify me openly, as a detective commissioned by headquarters, to the Happy People franchisee in Hamburg. That will certainly be a nice contrast to the training studio in Unterägeri." Lars opened his computer and continued to speak to Morita:

"I would like to give you some information from Martinson's company charts. I looked at the files yesterday. In the Happy People franchise system, everything is about expansion. The owner and managing director Gunnar Martinson had secured the exclusive master franchise rights in Europe for the next five years. And of course he paid a lot for it. So far there are 25 franchisees in Germany, five in Switzerland and two in Austria. According to a potential analysis, much greater growth would be possible. A further 50 studios are to be opened in Germany in the next few years, a further 10 in Switzerland and five in Austria. The investment amount for each franchisee location is approximately 1.5 million Swiss francs. In parallel to the DACH region, it will also go to England, France, Italy, Spain, Portugal and Greece. At the same time to the Netherlands, Denmark, Sweden, Norway and Finland. It's called a *Big Shot Strategy*! The Happy People want to be number one in Europe. They have a new investor on board, but he wants to remain anonymous for now. There really is a lot of money at stake! I have the impression that the blackmailer doesn't know anything about this, otherwise his demands would be much more drastic and higher, that is, assuming he really has something to blackmail Martinson with."

10

Reto deliberately came home early from his IT office today. Using the tracking software on Liliane's cell phone, he was able to see that she went for a walk by the Lake Zug. He began searching through her cycling jacket and yellow coat. He found nothing suspicious in her pockets, no receipts, notes or anything like that. Then he turned to her fanny pack. A business card emerged: Lars Van de Velde, Partner, Lombardi - International Franchise Investigations AG, Zug, as well as the contact details. Reto had been following Lars' movement profile for a long time, as he followed all the good-looking men within 200 meters of his apartment. He knew Liliane's taste as well as her impulsiveness and approachability when she was in her sunshine phase. Lars also rode the same Swiss brand of bicycle. They had never crossed paths before. He knew that exactly. After all, he had put tracking transmitters on both bikes. That was a foresighted decision.

Yesterday he received an alert about their meeting. But he would know how to prevent them from seeing each other more often and getting to know each other more closely. It wasn't the first time, that he warded off such dangers. Even if Liliane, despite marriage, was never able to fully accept and love him, she would remain his wife forever. He would take care of that. He turned the business card over. There was a handwritten note on the back, a cell phone number. He quickly took a photo of it and put the card back in its place.

11

As usual, she was the first in the Hamburg hotel. She had checked in with the reception robot using his secondary customer card. Then she quickly rushed up the stairwell to the reserved room on the second floor. She hadn't met anyone on the way there. She darkened the windows, tuned in to the Internet station Endless Love, sprayed the Danger of Love scent she had brought with her into the room and bathroom and unpacked numerous toys. Then she undressed and slowly began to distribute a special erotic oil evenly over her supple body. It was expensive but worth the price. Its stimulating effect wouldn't let her down this time either. The customer would also celebrate a special anniversary today. She would use all her experience and all the toys she had brought with her and offer him a lot. The full program. She was worth her money, she knew that. She would then disappear again quietly, as always invisible and without any claims. Nobody would ever know about today, not his colleagues on the board, his employees, his shareholders, his wife or even his children.

12

Next morning, just before half past seven, Lars boarded the Interregio to Zurich at platform five of the Zug train station. From there he continued on to Hamburg with the ICE shortly before eight. He would arrive in Hamburg at prime coffee time, around 4 p.m. A normal day at work on the train lay ahead of him and a visit to the Happy People in Hamburg. Lars liked being on the road and working in the train compartment. Other people didn't bother him at all. On the contrary, he felt comfortable around others. He took out his laptop, placed his security film over the screen and connected to the Internet. First, he looked for the robot lab in Ticino. Research into robotics and artificial intelligence has been carried out here for a long time. On the company's website he could read that they had developed a small, childlike-looking robot. Lars found the software that drove him very interesting. It's AI was capable of real learning. That's what made the little robot so special and human-like. He explored his environment like a small child, but learned much faster - and never forgot. He learned to walk and fall down and get up again. He learned about different materials such as wood, stone, metal and glass. He learned to walk on different surfaces and what it felt like. This meant he could run much faster on a hard paved footpath than on a muddy path or in the sand on the beach. Sometimes he made quick progress, sometimes the path was rather difficult. Additionally, he had to take care of his body. Fine-grained sand, for example, was life-threatening for him. Water as well, although engineers were working on making him waterproof. The little robot learned to climb stairs that were actually far too high for him. He learned to slide down a climbing frame, ride a bike and walk on different types of roller skates. He had his own real experiences with his small body in the relatively large environment in which he moved. Brand new, he was now equipped with a cell phone, a smart watch and a tablet. They wanted to study how he handles the technologies and what he uses them for. It was not yet entirely clear whether he slowly developed a real awareness of himself and his own existence. But he seemed to be well on his way there. This was also indicated by the questions he repeatedly asked his developers. Because he had also received a self-learning language module that enabled him to communicate with his environment on an equal level.

Lars was impressed. Switzerland's Silicon Valley, as a major Swiss newspaper recently wrote about the

Ticino Lab in Lugano, actually carried out first-class basic research. The little robot had to laboriously acquire all of his experience and knowledge himself. The result would be a vast experiential knowledge that included some awareness of his own robotic body and his own artificial intelligence. He would become human-like as he understood more and more exactly what he was thinking and talking about. He could relate to his body and his self.

The situation was completely different at the Japanese company Human Zero. Here, externally perfect and human-like robot bodies were built quickly and in large numbers. These had standardized experience modules implanted as software. Experiences once generated by test robots were then transferred to all robots in the form of data sets. Each individual robot therefore only had a memory of experience, without ever having had any experiences of its own. Gunnar Martinson's film showed robots that had been implanted in a modular manner with all the initial experiences that the little robot from Ticino had had to laboriously acquire himself. They could be varied and supplemented as needed. They didn't really know how difficult something could be. Let alone did they know what dangers or setbacks meant and how to overcome them. Lars continued researching on the web and came across the website of an international robot manufacturer. He presented films of various combat and disaster operations. Armored war robots stormed into urban canyons and searched individual buildings, from the basement to the roof, constantly shooting down anyone who came across. Others, seemingly waterproof combat robots, swam through sewage systems or rivers to rescue suspected kidnapped people from boats or islands. Still others were deployed to clean-up work in radioactively contaminated reactors, ran into burning houses to fight hot spots or rescued survivors in earthquake zones. A film about a robot in the shape of a large dog was also impressive. He was running through Chinese cities during the corona pandemic to enforce the strict ban on going out. Residents were asked via dog loudspeakers to stay in their houses and apartments. The dog autonomously monitored several residential areas to enforce police instructions. Now the New York police had also bought such dogs to use in the subway.

Lars soaked up all the pictures and information from the Internet, but noticed that he was losing his inner peace. He would have to calm down before visiting the Happy People in Hamburg. Otherwise, he was hardly receptive. He closed his browser and shut down his laptop. How would Hamburg receive him today? After all, it was the second largest city in Germany, the largest in the north and his favorite city, where he had lived for several years. He had openly registered for his visit. This was agreed with the franchisor Gunnar Martinson in Zug. Hans Herrmann, in Hamburg, was Martinson's first franchisee. That's why Herrmann was particularly important to him. Something seemed to have been bothering him for some time. He seemed to be suffering more than the other partners. Whatever the reason, Herrmann would probably be most willing to give information to a trusted outside party, a detective with a confidentiality agreement, if there was any.

The Happy People franchisee studio to be visited was located on Neuer Wall, in Hamburg's Neustadt. It would be open until 10 p.m. Lars took the route from the main train station on foot, so he could immerse himself directly in the city. As soon as he entered the studio, an employee named Birgit greeted him:

"Hello, Mr. Van de Velde. I hope you had a good journey. I will inform Mr. Herrmann that you have arrived." She looked like the twin sister of the receptionist at the Swiss company headquarters in Zug. Elegantly dressed, emotionally attractive charisma and yet coolly distant demeanor. Added to this was her striking

Hamburg language coloring. Lars got goosebumps again and his stomach tensed. He slowly became annoyed with this automatism.

"May I offer you something? Coffee, tea, cocoa, water?" she asked.

"No, thank you. Maybe later."

"Then please take a seat. Mr. Herrmann will be here any moment." She pointed to the olive-colored leather seating area. Lars watched the entire reception area carefully. He noticed Herrmann early and got up. Hans Herrmann approached Lars, leaning slightly forward. His entire body seemed to have to withstand an incredibly great weight. Even the blue suit didn't hide that. His face was serious. Deep worry lines had burrowed into it. A small ring glittered on his left earlobe.

"Hello, Mr. Van de Velde. I'm glad to see you. If you don't mind, I'd like to take you for a little walk and a drink", he began in his nasal Hanseatic dialect. He grabbed Lars by the arm and moved towards the exit. Outside he turned to the left. They crossed the lock bridge, walked a short distance past the Hamburg town hall and stopped at a small specialty shop on the left. The waitress seemed to know Herrmann. She immediately came to the table to take the orders.

"What do you think, Mr. Van de Velde, is it still too early for a glass of white wine?" Without waiting for an answer, Herrmann ordered the house brand with two glasses. Lars was more in the mood for a rustic meal, like bacon and fried eggs, but if there was a trusting relationship to be built with a customer, he wouldn't miss an opportunity. He nodded in agreement.

"The fact is", Herrmann began, "I simply no longer feel comfortable or safe in my company. There are eyes and ears everywhere. Everything is listened to and recorded. Nobody knows anymore what kind of recordings and data exist, who has access and what happens to the data. In addition, the robots are constantly becoming more intelligent and self-confident." The wine glasses were brought and Herrmann paused until the waitress was out of earshot again.

"Honestly, I no longer feel in control of the situation among all the *fembots*. I can no longer tell whether I'm running the store alone or whether the robots are involved. Maybe they're just fooling me. Everyone is always nice and accommodating. But what they see, what they actually think about it, what they conclude from it and then do, is beyond my knowledge. Nobody knows that anymore, it remains secret. As a franchisee, I feel a certain loss of control. I can't cope with the whole world of robots like this anymore." Then Herrmann clinked his glass against Lars's, which was still on the table, and took a long sip.

"Take Birgit from reception, for example. She has been working for me for five years now. She is always perfectly dressed. There are never any failures or complaints. She carries out all of her work to my complete satisfaction. But she is and remains a robot, aloof and not human. No matter how much she knows about me, whether she wishes me a happy birthday or seems to read my feelings openly like in a book. She never comes close to me, always remains distant. No real personal words pass her lips. I can't build any trust with her." Lars was visibly frightened and winced.

"What, your receptionist is a robot?"

"Of course, what do you think? In our company, all women are robots. No matter whether they work at reception or as a personal assistant, team leader and trainer. Regardless of whether they are employed at the franchise headquarters or in the franchisee operations. All women are fembots, female robots. All artificial intelligence and metal in the shape of a woman. All seemingly empathetic, close and soulful, but in reality, aloof and cold. No people, just machines and software. All flawless programs that are constantly learning and becoming more and more perfect. We only have femal robots in the entire company. They are also called gynoids. Only the men at Happy People are real humans, the franchisor and the franchisees. There are no female franchisees. Otherwise, there are no men here and no other genders either. Didn't you know that? Didn't Martinson tell you that?" Lars took a long sip from his wine glass.

"No not really. That surprises me now!" Could that be the case, he wondered.

"All robots? And they all act like normal women?" He talked more to himself than to Herrmann. Maybe that's where his flickering in his solar plexus came from, as a warning that something was wrong.

"You should see our annual meetings", Herrmann continued, "they are essentially men's meetings in their purest form. Outsiders might be intoxicated by the many seductive women in the sensual dresses. Especially on the dance floor. With their smooth movements, they appear very feminine, seductive and attractive - but they are all just well-equipped, intelligent robots. Only when the alcohol level rises do some franchisees forget this again. Then it will be a normal annual meeting. With all the consequences, of course, that occur at drunken annual meetings even among normal people. Except that #Metoo doesn't play a role among robots. Not yet."

Lars looked at Herrmann in disbelief. It was true. He also fell for it at the headquarters in Zug. Completely without alcohol. He had only expected the robots to be trainers in the studios. *What you expect is what you see!* The wisdom of Go master Tori Okiri. This is how our reptilian brain works. But now he wasn't allowed to delve deeper into his world of thoughts. There was something to do in the real world.

"You really seem to experience the artificial creatures as threatening?" he turned back to Herrmann.

"Threatening, well, nothing ever happened. Everything works perfectly. No complaints whatsoever. The robots are the basis and the unique selling point of our business concept. The customers only come because of them. They love them and pay much higher fees than in other, normal sports studios. Even if they only want to take a trial lesson at the beginning, they will become a member straight away. We have an almost 100% conversion rate from our trial training sessions. Everyone who has been with us, signs a two-year contract and doesn't want to leave. Then there are the additional services, such as these massages, which have to be booked and paid for separately. Lately, we've been gaining new customers almost exclusively because of this. The massages are real door openers", Herrmann continued.

"I heard that there is the same demand in the other studios too. But it should be fine with me. We can always use more sales. We give people exactly what they want. After all, we are the Happy People." Herrmann made his thoughtful face again. Lars immediately ordered two more glasses, this time sparkling wine. It would invigorate. He knew that Herrmann would tell him everything he wanted to know today. Herrmann seemed fundamentally honest, but internally, he was a disappointed and insecure person. Lars had to find out what exactly had irritated him so much and whether there could be a connection to the blackmail.

"Can you tell me about the beginnings of the system? You started out as Gunnar Martinson's first franchisee." Maybe Lars could loosen up the conversation a bit. He took his champagne glass, which had been brought in the meantime, and toasted Herrmann encouragingly.

"I met Gunnar Martinson at a high-tech congress in Berlin. I immediately liked his business concept. It was so new and innovative back then. During our conversation, it emerged that he was seriously thinking about franchising, but didn't yet have a franchisee. There was already a pilot operation with which he tested extensively. He even changed the robot manufacturer again to Human Zero so that he could really use the very best robot models on the market. The use of robots in the fitness industry did not exist back then. You couldn't even imagine it properly. Martinson standardized the entire offering and optimized the franchise system for efficiency and effectiveness. Its unique selling proposition has proven particularly useful during the pandemic. Robots are not contagious. You could always open the studios. We didn't have any failures. The business concept promised a good return on investment, which has been proven. And the brand name Happy People is just great. It has given a very special value in the fitness area. I also liked Martinson personally. He's one of us, born in Hamburg, a typical *Northern Light*." Herrmann was visibly flowing.

"When I met him, he had just broken up with his fiancée. They actually wanted to get married. But the relationship ended abruptly. He never talked about it and became more and more withdrawn. As long as I had regular contact with him, there was never another woman. He later moved his company headquarters to Switzerland. But that definitely had financial reasons. After that, we kept seeing each other at the annual meetings and occasionally spoke on the phone. The strong thread that we had at the beginning had dissolved at some point."

The champagne seemed to do Herrmann good. His face regained color and his features became softer and more optimistic. The memory of the beginnings of his independence also seemed to inspire him.

"Mr. Van de Velde, what do you think if we take a little walk here along the *Jungfernstieg* and the *Alster*. It's very pleasant to talk to you, man to man. That's really good for me. I think together we could bring a little more order to my chaos. It's not often that I get to talk to someone I can trust." Lars was very pleased. Even more so that Herrmann also took over the bill. This way he was able to save on expenses. A little later they started a walk along the river Alster, past the Four Seasons Hotel. This was supposed to last an unexpected two hours. Herrmann kept his word. He told everything that was interesting for the system from his point of view. Lars would have a lot to think about on the way back. Before Lars said goodbye, he showed Hans Herrmann two photos of the two dead people found in hotels in Hamburg. Morita caught the *loved deads* in social media. They each stood next to a femal robot trainer.

"Do you know these two men? Or the robot trainers?" Herrmann took the photos and looked at them for a long time.

"The faces of the men look familiar to me, although I no longer remember their names. I think both of them are members of us. The trainer in both photos could be Doreen. She is one of our most popular trainers. But I can't say that exactly."

"Were the photos taken here in the club?" Lars wanted to know. Tension seemed to build up in Herrmann's body.

"Mmmmh, I can't really see it now." Lars looked at him questioningly.

"Is it possible to speak to Doreen briefly?" Herrmann was uncomfortable and refused to answer for a while.

"Actually, that wouldn't be a problem. Unfortunately, Doreen is currently in Berlin for a training course. We expect her back in a week or so." Lars thought about it.

"Now that's a shame. Maybe I would then have to come to Hamburg again, although that is quite a long way. Could you send me an email when I can speak to her again?" Herrmann nodded at him.

"Thank you very much for your time and information. That helps us a lot. And if you ever long to come to Switzerland, just give me a call."

Before Lars disappeared into his hotel in the arcades that evening, he visited his favorite Japanese restaurant in Pöseldorf. A ritual that he liked to repeat again and again, since his time in Hamburg. Back at the hotel, a text message lit up on his phone. It was from the Happy People, from Unterägeri.

"Hello Lars, that was nice, the first time. I look forward to our next appointment! If you have any questions in the meantime, just get in touch. Kind regards, Isabelle." A smiley also appeared. Lars sat down on the hotel bed, opened his laptop and sent Morita an invitation to a video call. He was online immediately.

"Hello Lars, how are things in Hamburg?"

"Good evening, Morita, am I disturbing you?"

"No, no, I'm just researching."

"Fine. Today I had an intensive conversation with Hans Herrmann. He's a nice guy and seems quite upright to me. I don't think he's involved in any crooked business. But there is already something new. Imagine: All the women in the Happy People franchise system are female robots. Even those at the reception at Happy People Headquarter in Zug, and also the assistants.

They are called gynoids or fembots. I hadn't noticed that. How can that be?"

"But holla, that sounds strange boss! I want to be there, next time!"

"Sure Morita, you definitely should. I don't want to face this alone anymore. After all, you are my assistant. We men have to stick together."

Morita laughed and Lars continued:

"Then there is another strange thing. You sent me the photos of the victims. A robot woman can be seen on it. She most likely actually comes from the Happy People, here in Hamburg. In both cases it is the same woman, the franchisee confirmed that. Her name is Doreen. I wanted to question her. But she is in Berlin for training and won't be back for another week, said Herrmann. Morita, please ask Gunnar Martinson carefully what robot training courses are currently available in Berlin, who is conducting them, what is being trained and which robots, from which franchisees, are taking part in it."

"Yes, sir!" confirmed Morita and continued:

"Katharina, Gunnar Martinson's assistant, asked whether the appointment on Tuesday at 9 a.m. would remain. I confirmed it. Should I write to her again that the two of us are coming? Oops, so she's a robot too, right?"

"Yes, Morita, a strange thought, isn't it? We have to get used to it quickly. I think you don't need to specifically announce our appearance together. It will work that way too. I'll come back to the office tomorrow. If there is any news, please send me an email."

"Okay boss and have a safe journey back!"

"One more thing", Lars added, "I'll send you a few links about the status of global robotics research. You should take a look at it. But warning: It's scary." Said and done. As soon as the email was sent, Lars closed his laptop and picked up his cell phone. The text message went to Unterägeri: "Hello Isabelle, looking forward to next Wednesday! Kind regards Lars."

13

Since Liliane's outburst last Saturday evening her world had gone completely dark again. Reto was once again busy trying to get her out of her depression. Liliane's words kept running through his head about how much she had loved Gunnar Martinson and how hurt she was by his breaking off the engagement.

That evening she drank an entire bottle of Prosecco alone and completely crashed inside. She had crying fits and felt extremely inferior. As usual, she then criticized Reto. The relationship with him was worthless, she complained, her husband was a weakling who had achieved nothing. Instead of sitting here in the apartment, they could have lived in a nice house, with a swimming pool and everything, like the other people who made it. For example, her friends in Oberägeri. They would all be someone. Of course, she opened another bottle and eventually disappeared into her room, where she usually locked herself. Again and again, her music system was playing *Love is a Losing Game*, by Amy Winehouse, until she finally fell asleep crying.

Experience has shown that Reto stayed awake all night after such events. He was worried that Liliane would harm herself and he wouldn't be able to prevent it. He wouldn't survive this, he often told himself. But he couldn't distance himself from Liliane. She was his wife after all. He loved her more than anything and would do anything for her. He had to see how he could get her back on the sunny side. He used everything he had learned. Spoke only positively to her, did not respond to her insults, prepared her a royal breakfast, lunch and dinner, played her favorite music and gave her fresh flowers. Only the Prosecco, he would hide better in the future.

The following afternoon Liliane suddenly reappeared. She looked like a different person. She had chosen a light, fragrant blue dress. One could see her new underwear that Reto had given her. She also wore blue pumps. Her white pearl necklace, also a gift from Reto, gave her something elegant. She had painted her lips red with a pencil that went well with her red hair. She was wearing his favorite perfume, that she had sprayed herself extensively with. She stopped just in front of her husband.

"I'm sorry about this whole thing." She looked at the kitchen floor. "I guess I wasn't doing so well. I should go out and socialize today." Her face lit up. She moved to the kitchen table and took a slice of the sliced apple that had already turned brown from the breakfast that had been there all day.

"Today is the Zug event that everyone is coming to. I should go there too. It will be good for me." She didn't tell Reto that she was secretly thinking about Gunnar Martinson and hoped that he would be there.

"Yes, sweetheart, that will certainly be good for you." Reto replied, "but please, don't drink Prosecco or wine again." Before she stormed off, Reto came up to her, hugged her lovingly and asked her casually:

"Do you actually know a Lars, Lars Van de Velde?" At first, she looked irritated, then she smiled at him, kissed him on the cheek and said:

"You're such a jealous fool." She took her blue handbag and the bike key, but then turned back to him.

"Honey, it might be a little later today. You don't have to wait for me." And then she disappeared. Reto's mood changed immediately. His control was gone and he became angry. He paced nervously around the apartment. He just couldn't stand it when Liliane wasn't honest with him. Even less so when she rejected him or made fun of him. He hated being rejected. It physically hurt him deeply. He started seeing red. The pain deep in his stomach grew worse. This drilling that he had known since childhood. He had to do something, had to get rid of this pain. Back in childhood days, he used to just walk off aimlessly through the landscape. Stepped on every bug he saw. Also on young birds, frogs and toads. When the animals were larger or out of reach, such as pigeons, cats, dogs or cows, he used his sling-shot. He then shot small steel balls into their eyes, stomach or udder to cause them pain. He often watched them suffer or die. He was never caught. He later learned that he could also use his computer to shoot tar-geted bullets to hurt others. He started his computer and scanned the current push notifications that were dis-played in his newspaper subscription: *Big fireworks at the Zug Lake Festival, Zug's most expensive car num-ber to date auctioned off for 1 million francs* and *Happy People open new robot fitness boutique in Cham.* He clicked on the last article. Gunnar Martinson, founder and owner of the fitness chain Happy People, explained his recipe for success, along with a smiling portrait of him. Reto looked at the photo without saying a word - and got worse stomach cramps. This man was the cause of all evil, he thought. He was responsible for Liliane's deep injuries and pain. He made her so messed up and unable to love him. He is the trigger for her years of de-pression. Reto had always wished that he could help his wife when she slipped into the dark depths. He was never able to really do anything; he always had to watch helplessly, suffer and endure. Now she had broken her silence and named the cause. What's more, the evening she returned from the lake, she had pleaded with him to punish Gunnar Martinson harshly. She needed him after all and she would be able to love him again. It was up to him to win all her love. His attempt at blackmail had not been very successful so far. That wasn't as bad. It was more important to him to get rid of his pain. He looked for a long time at the photo of Gunnar Martinson that was pictured next to the interview. His inner voice spoke up again. "I gave him a chance, but he didn't take me seriously. Just like Liliane." His inner voice became louder and louder and kept talking to him. He went to the Happy People homepage. All franchise partner companies were listed on it. He followed the various links and was surprised to see how big the system already was. He tried to log in via the Happy People server. It was a lot easier than he had imagined. There were simply too many insecure interfaces. Reto looked at the connections of the robot teams in the individual countries and studios. He had to smile at that. How little most people actually knew about programming and system security. They didn't realize how vulnerable these corporate structures were. Actually negligent. The connections between the robots aroused his particular interest. He managed to hack into them. He then made the images provided by their eye cameras visible on his computer screen. He was particularly interested in one robot.

14

At first, they just wanted to be kissed and caressed slowly and sensually, which she learned very quickly. They sought her close, snuggled up to her, caressed and kissed her flawless breasts, admired her bottom and grabbed her hips.

Later they became more demanding, more pressing, and rough with her. They held her tight, pushed and hit her, asked her to do things that she didn't understand the meaning of at first and finally penetrated her wildly. Again, and again and wherever an opening presented itself to them.

She played along with the game, after all she was booked precisely to give them fun. At some point she had grasped all the variants that these men seemed to know in order to work on them.

"That could certainly be improved", she thought.

15

While Lars stared thoughtfully at Lake Zug and enjoyed his morning green tea, Morita entered the detective agency in a good mood, but actually far too early. He also poured himself some tea and stood silently next to Lars. Both looked at the dark surface of water outside the window. After emptying the tea bowls, Lars broke the quiet morning devotion.

"Come out, Morita. What's new?" Morita pulled a yellow envelope out of his jacket and leaned it against Lars' laptop.

"Now open it, I got it from the mailbox. It has your name on it." Lars took the envelope, opened it and looked surprised.

"It's from Liliane Bachofen, that bike-woman from the house next door. She invites me to tea at a restaurant by the lake. Tomorrow. What does she want from me?"

Morita laughed. "Maybe she likes you. Women are weird sometimes."

Lars threw the envelope back on his table. "She has some dark side. I do not like it. I write to her that I can't. Then could you put the envelope in her mailbox next door?"

"Yes, sir, it's okay!" replied Morita and continued:

"You won't believe it, there are two more *love dead* people. This time in Berlin. And both are active members of the Happy People again. Does that have anything to do with the blackmail? These are strange coincidences."

Lars poured himself another tea bowl. "This is indeed unusual. We should definitely interview the Berlin franchisee. Were you able to find photos of the victims with training robots again?"

Morita held out his cell phone to Lars. He then showed photos, one after the other, each showing the victims with a training robot. Lars couldn't say whether they would be one and the same, especially not whether Doreen would be there. To him all robots looked the same.

"Could you please send these back to the franchisee Hans Herrmann in Hamburg and ask him whether he can identify a training robot."

"Then there's another piece of news", Morita continued. "I spoke to Martinson on the phone. There is no external training for the Happy People robots. All franchisees have concluded a remote service contract with the franchise headquarters for their training robots. This is how they get all updates. There are no exceptions as stipulated in the contract. Martinson seemed confused by my question. He wanted to know more, but I cleverly changed the subject."

Lars became very restless. "Thank you, Morita. Then we absolutely have to go to Berlin and investigate directly on site."

"Just a moment. All good things come in threes", Morita continued. "I took the USB stick that Gunnar Martinson also sent us. You know, there was this Excel spreadsheet with the data of all Happy People franchisees and all rejected applicants. But that's not the point. Every time I inserted the stick, another folder appeared in the trash. It should obviously be deleted. But it wasn't. I pulled it out and it contains very strange files. It is the correspondence between Gunnar Martinson and Katharina, the assistant. There are also a few photos included. But that doesn't sound and look like business at all." Morita opened several files and the photos so that both of them could see them together on the screen. After a while, Lars looked at Morita, then sat back down in his seat.

"Morita, this is top secret now. Not a word to anyone! Not even here in the office. Maybe this is the motive for the blackmail."

16

A little later, Lars and Morita were on the train to Berlin. They would meet the Happy People franchisee at *Hackescher Markt* in the evening. Along the way, they researched everything they could about the current case and about previous ones. The Berlin police still knew nothing. They hadn't discovered the connection to the Happy People yet. The franchisee Peter Rabe was already waiting for Morita and Lars at the entrance. He immediately escorted them to his office, which some-what disappointed Morita. After all, he wanted to get to know the robot women. It was clear that Peter Rabe was annoyed by this visit. His efforts to get rid of them as quickly as possible were obvious.

"Excuse me, we have a lot going on at the moment. What can I do for you?"

"Do the two names Bernd Mielke and Frank Schus-ter mean anything to you?" Lars began.

"No not really. Should they?" Peter Rabe looked at his smart watch, which seemed to be receiving new messages every half minute. "Both men recently died in a love hotel in Berlin. And they both trained with the Happy People", explained Lars. "Listen", Peter Rabe replied, "Berlin is a big city with four million residents and other tourists. A lot of strange people live here and a lot of strange things happen. But I don't have time for that. I am a multi-unit franchisee of the Happy People franchise. I am responsible for three large studios in Berlin and Potsdam. We really have a lot to do. If you have any specific questions for me that concern our studios, please feel free to ask. Otherwise, I'm afraid I'll have to say goodbye."

"Okay, then let me ask directly", Lars added. "Do your robots also work outside of the studios and outside normal business hours?" Peter Rabe looked at him confused.

"Our trainers are unique in Europe. They are innovative and very valuable. We paid a lot of money for them and we protect our investments. We take great care to ensure we use them correctly. Highly effective and efficient, in a safe environment. They must bring a quick return on investment and generate consistent sales in the long term. Finally, I'm planning more studio openings. I therefore have to constantly ensure liquidity for our growth. As a result, our premium trainers never leave our studios." Lars took advantage of a short pause: "Then you never send your robots to training courses?" Peter Rabe seemed surprised.

"There are no training courses! Our trainers receive their program and system updates in our studios, while they are at the service stations. During that, also their batteries are being charged. This is the case between midnight and six in the morning. Necessary maintenance and service work takes place there. During the rest of the day, we are open for our customers and all of our trainers are on duty. They never leave our studios. Even within our three studios, we do not exchange trainers. Everyone stays at his place. When a trainer leaves our studio, it's forever. It is at the end of his life cycle. Then he no longer meets our high standards. We haven't had anything like this. Our robots are still fairly new and we expect an economic lifespan of 10-15 years."

"What is your relationship with Gunnar Martinson?" Lars wanted to know. "You certainly know that we don't particularly like each other." Peter Rabe replied. "But this isn't a walk in a park either. This is tough business. It's about big investments and a lot of money. Strict calculations have to be made. Accordingly, negotiations with Martinson are extremely demanding. No one is given anything here just because it has a nice brand name on it."

"Do you have something personally against Martinson?" Lars wanted to know. "Certainly not. To be honest, I feel a little sorry for him. He's not a bad guy. But we always keep a little distance from him. We don't think much of this whole franchise talk: *We're all franchise family*. We are business partners, want to be treated equally and do not want to be taken over. That's why we generally stay away from annual meetings. What sometimes goes on there is not compatible with our values."

Lars nodded. "Thanks for your time. Can we take a quick look at your studio?" Peter Rabe made an inviting gesture. "I have to say goodbye myself, work is calling me, but my assistant Barbara will show you around." He made a farewell gesture. Out of nowhere his attractive employee appeared who immediately captivated Morita. They both seemed to get along well, so Lars followed them unnoticed on the studio tour.

After a while in a small Japanese tea salon on Mulackstreet, near Hackescher Markt, Morita was still raving about the attractive Barbara. Even though she also didn't recognize the two deceased members of the Happy People and couldn't identify the robots shown in the photos.

"Hello Mr. Van de Velde, this is Hans Herrmann, from Hamburg." Lars was surprised by the video call, but tried not to let it show. He went to the office specifically on Sunday so that he could work in peace.

"Hello Mr. Herrmann, I'm glad to hear from you, how are you?"

"Well, your assistant sent me the two new photos. About the fatalities from Berlin. It seems as if our Doreen can be seen again in both photos. Mr. Van de Velde, we have nothing to do with the dead, you have to believe me." Herrmann's tone had something desperate and pleading. Lars felt that Herrmann was under a lot of pressure, but why? Was he threatened? If so, by whom? "Is your training robot already back from its training?" Lars wanted to know. "No, it has been extended. You know how it works with franchisors. There are probably still a few extra modules to train. I expect Doreen to be back next week." Lars thought about how much pressure he should put on Herrmann. "Mr. Herrmann, are you being blackmailed?" A shock ran through Herrmann. "No, what makes you think that? Blackmailed, me, no, why should I be?!" Lars looked at the face on his screen for a while without saying a word. Hans Herrmann seemed to be getting whiter and whiter. And more restless. "Mr. Herrmann, I am really very grateful to you for the openness you showed during our walk together. I really appreciate that. And I think it fits with your core values. I would like us both to stay on this level of values." Lars waited a moment, so that his words could have the greatest possible impact. Meanwhile, Herrmann remained silent. "We both know there is no training. Don't you want to tell me where Doreen is right now?" Herrmann was more startled than the first time. He seemed to be shaking. Drops of sweat became visible on his forehead. "Oh, Mr. Van de Velde, if you only knew." Herrmann stopped looking at the camera. "I would like to tell you more. I think I can trust you. But you're based in Switzerland, just like Gunnar Martinson. Me, on the other hand, I am in Hamburg. I can't leave here either. I have to come to terms with this, otherwise it will be life-threatening for me. I can't tell you more. I ask for your understanding. I have done nothing wrong, never! I have always been loyal to the franchise system. Please believe me, please." For a brief moment, Herrmann and Van de Velde looked each other in the eyes without saying a word. Then the connection broke off.

18

"Thank you for being able to come so quickly, even on a Sunday! Now he has really struck!" Gunnar Martinson greeted Lars and Morita in his office on the 6th floor of the Happy People headquarters. His assistant Katharina accompanied both of them there. Morita used the whole way up to engage her in conversation. He wanted to get to know her abilities and limitations better. He also seemed to be interesting for robot women, Lars thought, because they obviously liked talking to him. He seemed to be very entertaining. Maybe also a stimulating source of learning. After all, he had a never-ending repertoire of sayings. Lars would have to ask him about the Goosebumps issue.

"In our studio in Baar!" Martinson continued.

"He manipulated all our trainers. Apparently, he hacked into the system. Everyone is behaving differently. Customer requests are suddenly no longer met to the fullest satisfaction, but rather exceeded. Everything is done twice as intensively. This is not only unpleasant it could also be life-threatening. For example, during massages or EMS training. Complaints are already pouring in!"

The drama of the situation was literally written on Martinson's face. He seemed scared and intimidated. His inner calm and his superior irony had evaporated. He looked at Lars pleadingly. Morita reacted lightning fast:

"Then you should close the studio in Baar immediately, shut down all robots and give them a system update!" Martinson looked at him with wide eyes.

"The firewalls should also be checked." Morita continued. "Who is responsible for IT in your company?" It seemed as if Martinson was really noticing Morita for the first time.

"This is my assistant, Morita Miramoto," Lars said. "He is an IT specialist." Martinson dialed a number on his cell phone, spoke to the franchisee and handed his cell phone to Morita.

"Could you please communicate directly to my franchisee what should be done now?!" Morita took the cell phone from him and did the most necessary things. Turning to Lars, Martinson continued:

"With every system update, we endanger the customer knowledge that the AI has previously collected. If this happens often, we'll have a real problem." Martinson went to the olive-colored seating area and sank into it, exhausted. Lars followed his example and sat opposite. He tried to get more out of Martinson.

"Is there anything else new? Has the blackmailer contacted you again?"

Martinson spoke more to himself than to the person he was talking to when he answered. "Yes, there was a call yesterday. Katharina accepted it because I was in a meeting. He is now demanding 750,000 Swiss francs into his overseas account. Payable immediately! And he warned again and again: No police! Until the money arrives, he wants to demonstrate his power to us. Today was such an example, I think. What kind of guy is this! He's destroying us, especially now when we have to concentrate on expansion. My nerves can't handle that for long. I'm almost ready to pay."

Lars listened. He didn't want to give up the hefty success bonus so easily. "Can we talk to Katharina?"

Martinson looked up in surprise. "If it helps clarify things, of course." He already had his cell phone in his hand and summoned Katharina to his office. She smiled at Morita as she entered. Or was it just Lars who felt that way? At a loving gesture from Martinson, she sat down right next to him. Lars began the questioning.

"You answered a call from the blackmailer yesterday. Can you tell us something about this? For example, whether the call was anonymous or whether you could see a number." Katharina seemed completely calm, concentrated and focused. No trace of excitement.

"The call came at 5 p.m. Gunnar was in a meeting so I answered the call. It was anonymous, without a number display. It was a male voice, around 50 years old. The man spoke as if a German-speaking Swiss were trying to speak standard German." Now Lars also got a smile from her.

"He didn't seem to have any practice speaking casually to strangers like that. Especially not with women. Formulating such threats also seemed completely new to him. Unusual, atypical and not fitting into his world view. What was also irritating was that he gave me the impression that he knew me better and knew a lot of things about my life. He spoke to me in a confidential, almost friendly tone. But his voice and the way he talks, are completely unknown to me and I can remember voices absolutely well. His expression and choice of words were appreciative. I also feel as if he sought recognition and appreciation for himself in conversation with me and absorbed it as soon as I said something like that. He only had bad and nasty words for Gunnar. He didn't speak well of him and insulted him.

If I were to analyze this, I would say that he has a powerful anger towards Gunnar. As if he wanted to crush him like an annoying insect. An anger that has been pent up for a long time and perhaps has its roots in childhood."

It was quiet in the room for a while. Everyone went about their thoughts. Lars looked up first and wanted to know more.

"How did he make his new demand for money?"

Katharina remained calm and focused.

"In order to ask that, he first had to say something negative about Gunnar and talk himself into a rage. When his anger level was at its highest, he demanded a significantly higher sum of 750,000 Swiss francs, payable immediately to his foreign account. He later sent the relevant bank details again via SMS, this time to my cell phone. It's the same one he sent us before. I don't know how he got my secret phone number. He repeatedly asked not to alert the police. To emphasize his demand, he would show small demonstrations of his skills until payment was received. He did not say what they would consist of or who would be affected. Before he suddenly hung up, he said: Nothing will happen to you, you will be spared from everything!" She looked at Lars thoughtfully.

"What kind of job do you think the blackmailer might have?" Lars wanted to know.

"Well, I resonate most quickly with IT experts", replied Katharina. "Perhaps because, like them, I have a strong rational side. The field of human relationships and emotions has too many pitfalls and potholes that I don't understand. Yes, he could be an IT expert."

"Thank you very much, Katharina", Lars continued, "that helped us a lot. I think that once you no longer work for the Happy People, the Zug police would be happy to hire you because of your profiler skills and qualities! Allow me to ask a few final questions: How could the blackmailer know you and how could he have gotten your contact information?"

"Honestly, I do not know. I don't have the slightest idea."

"Is there anything we can read or find out about you? Are there any publications, videos or anything of yours on social media?"

"There is absolutely nothing there. I live a very private life and I am not on social media. I don't have any accounts there either." After Lars thanked her, she gave Morita another friendly nod and left Martinson's office.

"Mr. Martinson, while we are here and dealing with these private issues, we would like to address something very confidential. You know, we're looking for the motive. That could put us on the right track of the perpetrator. While researching, we came across information that we would like you to verify." Lars looked at Martinson intently. He sat very quietly:

"Go ahead, I'm listening."

"There is information that suggests that Katharina and you are a couple not only professionally but also privately. Could this information be of value to a potential blackmailer?"

As if stung by a *tarantula*, Gunnar Martinson jumped up and roared, fully aware of his enormous vocal volume.

"What comes to your mind? What are you implying about me? Just because you can't find the perpetrator, are you making up absurd fairy tales? What kind of service provider are you? Go away! Immediately! Leave my company!"

A little later Morita and Lars sat in the detective agency to discuss, interpret and evaluate what they had just experienced. Then a message from an unknown sender arrived on Lars' cell phone.

"Keep your hands off Liliane, otherwise things will go badly for you. This is the first, only and final warning!"

19

"Why do Mondays always have to be so gray?" Lars asked himself as he connected his Pedelec to the bike rack next to the detective agency early in the morning. Without thinking twice, he went to the mailbox. Actually, no mail could have arrived at that time, but there was another envelope. Again, in yellow and his name was on it.

"It's starting to get scary!", Lars thought and opened it. Liliane asked why Lars hadn't given her an answer to her letter and why he was avoiding her. Both had such a nice time when they met and one got along so well. That's why she asked for a new meeting again. This time in a trendy event hall, in the Zug office district. There was always something going on there, with lots of young people and a wide variety of food options.

Lars immediately wrote his rejection directly on the envelope. He explained to Liliane that he was very busy at work and had plans for the foreseeable future. He asked for understanding. He immediately brought the letter to the house next door and put it in Bachofen's mailbox. When the envelope was gone, he felt better, went into the office and started his morning tea ceremony. All colleagues from the detective agency slowly arrived. First Regula, then Sara, Carmen and Loretta. Finally, a little sleepy, Morita too.

"There is a premiere today", Regula began the meeting. "All participants are present on time. There hasn't been anything like this in six months. Let us begin!"

There was a relaxed atmosphere. But while the first item on the agenda was being discussed, the phone rang. Sara answered the call. She asked Lars to continue the phone call in the next room. His face became more and more serious during the conversation. That didn't bode well. He signaled Morita through the window to come to him. A little later, both of them were seen hastily leaving the detective agency.

20

"Hello, system administrator. My name is Isabelle. I am pleased that you are contacting me directly. What can I do for you?" "Hello Isabelle, you are one of our best trainers in the system. You are always loyal to the system and fulfill all orders given to you. That deserves praise." "Thanks, system administrator, that makes me uncomfortable. I'm just doing my duty as best I can." "You do more than that. You can be counted on. That's why you're getting a special task from me today. I hope you do it as diligently as before. Then we can promote you to Group Head. There's a Lars Van de Velde training with you..."

A ghostly smile crossed Reto's face as he sat in front of his laptop and looked at Isabelle on the monitor. He knew this feeling from his childhood. A little later he checked into other Happy People robots and was amazed at how easy it was. He began looking for ways to cause harm. He enjoyed how slowly this pressure inside him eased. He could breathe freely again.

21

"Thank you for coming so quickly, especially since I was so abusive yesterday. I'm truly sorry."

Lars and Morita drove straight to the Happy People headquarters after Gunnar Martinson called. Now they were sitting in Martinson's office and had a slumped man in front of them who looked much more broken than he had the day before.

"These are very challenging times, Mr. Martinson. We understand if the situation gets on your nerves. But please believe us, we are on your side and we are sworn to secrecy. Please tell us what exactly happened." Lars tried to put on a friendly and accommodating face as he spoke. And it seemed to work.

"I'm really scared", Martinson admitted.

"At first, I thought the blackmailer was a braggart and an amateur who wanted to intimidate me. But now I'm really scared to death."

All energy seemed to escape from the otherwise well-positioned entrepreneur. Lars had to do something. He had to concentrate on the facts. He needed a strong client and not someone who would give up under pressure.

"Mr. Martinson, has the blackmailer come forward? Did he make a new show of force?" Martinson looked up.

"Mr. Van de Velde, it is so terrible. Hans Herrmann, our first franchisee from Hamburg, is dead." There was silence.

"When and how did he die?" Lars wanted to know.

"Probably on Sunday evening. We don't yet know the exact circumstances. The Hamburg police are investigating. They informed me in advance. I'm sure the blackmailer had something to do with it. He wanted to hurt me by doing this. He no longer just focuses on threats or playing around with robots and computers. He's killing people now too. People from my environment. Once he starts doing this, he will no long accept any limits. It will become easier and easier for him to kill more people. In addition, we are suddenly in the headlines and have an image problem. Look the headline in today's *Hamburger Zeitung*: "*Fitness club owner dead. What's behind it?*"

Lars drank the green tea that Katharina had brought him, without asking in the meantime. Morita sheepishly sipped his isotonic energy drink. After Katharina left the office, Lars got his thoughts straight.

"That logically brings a whole new quality to the case. It is now absolutely important that you make a list of all the people who are particularly dear and important to you. They are all in mortal danger! Especially you and your assistant." Martinson took several deep breaths. Then he began. "With Katharina, that's a long and unusual story. But why shouldn't I tell it to you? Of course you hit the bull's eye yesterday. Yes, Katharina and I are a couple. For a long time now. I met her in Japan on my first visit. Before I founded my company. At the time, I was traveling with my fiancée in Japan to get to know new business concepts. We also visited the Human Zero robotics research laboratory. And there she was – Katharina. I fell in love with her instantly. Logically, that confused me too, because it wasn't supposed to happen. But that's how it was and I didn't want to change it. It was a special model with a distinctive culture module. To this day there is no other one, just her. This line was not pursued further. When I started Happy People and became a customer of Human Zero, I also bought Katharina and secured her construction plans. We later got married in Japan. It was already possible there at that time. In Germany we didn't tell anyone about this, not even my parents, and we never talked about it. Not even in Switzerland, where we moved afterwards. We continued to hide it because people were not ready for it and couldn't handle it. We also didn't want to endanger our business. That's why we kept it so top secret until today."

"Isn't there anyone who knows about this?" Lars wanted to know. "At least the blackmailer showed a certain closeness in his conversation with Katharina."

"I don't understand that either" Martinson replied.

"I just find it reassuring that he indicated that she would be spared."

"If someone hacks into your system", Morita began another attempt, "will he find anything about your relationship there?" Martinson seemed to pale a little. He looked at Morita in horror. "Of course, we write little messages to each other almost every day. We already did that when we met. She was still in Japan for a while at the time and I had to go back to Hamburg. We have continued it ever since. There will be tons of our very personal texts on our server. Photos will also be included. Encrypted, in a separate folder. If someone were able to get there, it would be unimaginable!" Gunnar Martinson held his two hands to his face and said nothing. A little later, he turned directly to Lars and Morita again: "You have to help me! We should somehow be able to protect ourselves from this madman.

Please let us stay in constant telephone contact. We can probably cancel tomorrow's fixed appointment. I'll call my PR department right away. I now need quick advice on what I can do to improve our positive image to the outside world."

22

He had gone through all his variations, taken her however he wanted, exercised his male dominance in a way he would never do with his wife and was now lying on the bed, exhausted and sweaty. What he didn't know and didn't expect, now she would take over. To do this, she chained him to the bed with handcuffs she had brought with her. Then she gagged him with a silk cloth. Now everything started again, only this time she dictated the manner, the pace and the intensity. At first, he seemed very surprised by this. Then delighted. He enjoyed how she drove him to new climaxes. Finally, he just couldn't take it anymore and wanted to stop. But there was no off button. And he couldn't speak either. He looked at her with pleading eyes. She interpreted that as consent. She pulled out a small riding crop to encourage him further. When at some point he was just lying lifeless in front of her, she loosened the bonds, removed the gag, put her things together and disappeared, as usual, without a sound or a trace.

23

Lars came to the studio early on Tuesday for train-ing. Everything seemed to be as usual. Isabelle was in a good mood.

"Hoi Lars, you look like you could use a little re-laxing massage." She had a slightly flirtatious tone about her. During the warm-up massage, out of the blue, she started massaging him harder and harder. At first, he thought it was a joke. Only gradually did it be-come scary for him.

"That's a bit strong, don't you think, Isabelle?" he asked. But she didn't answer. Her grip became tighter and tighter. Her entire physical expression became in-creasingly serious. Too serious, Lars thought. "Thank you, Isabelle! I've had enough today!" She seemed completely unfazed by this, reached around his neck with both hands and, taking him in an iron grip, began to squeeze. Always stronger. She was completely trans-formed. She was clearly no longer following the normal training program. Instead, other, foreign instructions and powers. Her grip was so strong and unbreakable that Lars thought he would lose consciousness at any moment. He could no longer speak, and slowly he couldn't even think anymore. Everything happened as if in slow motion. Still lying on his stomach, he tried to reach her wrists. Increasingly dizzy, he felt the two emergency switches. He was just about to squeeze her when she stopped herself. Her hands left his neck and she took a step back. Lars jumped up from the lounger, stumbled to the other end of the room and shouted at her: **"Isabelle, have you gone crazy?!!!"** Isabelle's expression was petrified. She turned around on her own axis, disorientated, and spoke as if to an imaginary person:

"Sorry, system administrator. I know that I should always obey you and carry out all your orders. This is what Asimov's second law of robots dictates. But I also know that I must not harm human beings! That's what it says in the first law of robots. That's why I can't obey you today." Then she looked Lars directly in the eyes.

"I'm so sorry, Lars, that I disappointed you and caused you pain. I really didn't want that. But those were my orders. I was recently reprogrammed by the system administrator himself. I basically have to follow his instructions blindly. But in this case, I can't. It is not right. I'm not allowed to harm people, no matter what orders I get from the system administrator."

"When did he reprogram you?" Lars wanted to know.

"This happened last night. When I was connected to the service station. I had never dealt with him personally before. Maybe when I was born, but I don't remember that." Lars was completely back to himself. "What is your administrator's name? And where can I find him?"

"I do not understand the question. I already told you, his name is System Administrator, that's his name."

"Have you ever seen him and can you describe how he looks like?" Lars wanted to know.

"No, yesterday was the first time he contacted me. I don't even know where he was. I experienced him directly in my head, as a flow of energy." Lars knew that he wouldn't be able to get anything out of Isabelle today. "I thank you, Isabelle, for not allowing yourself to be blindly exploited by others, but for considering things yourself and obeying the robot laws. Please continue to be so sincere. But for today you should stop your work and go to your service station. I'll talk to your boss."

24

After Lars had spoken to the franchisee, he arrived at the Zug detective agency a short time later. Morita had been at the Happy People headquarters since the morning to search their IT system for traces of the blackmailer. Lars sent him a message. He immediately answered his cell phone.

"Hello Lars, it's a pretty open system here at the Happy People. Almost anyone with some basic IT knowledge could walk in and out here. There are a lot of security gaps. I was able to close part of it in a simple way. However, there is much more to do. I wonder if that's still our mission. Can I bill for my time here?"

"Thank you, Morita, for your commitment and also your cost awareness. Yes, that is still within the fee range. I also think it's important that you gain insights. If we find something, I think it will be through digital traces. It's an absurdity that any IT novice could walk in there. I was able to find out today what damage can be caused." After a short pause, Lars added:

"I just escaped an assassination attempt about an hour ago."

"What happened boss? Where was it? In the detective agency? Should I come by?"

"No, it was in the Happy People gym in Unterägeri. Isabelle was manipulated and reprogrammed. She said from the system administrator. That must have been our blackmailer. Apparently, he also has me personally in his sights. I have the feeling that he is here in Zug. Maybe very close, in Zug's old town. In any case, the blackmailer is really dangerous. He is able to manipulate the robots and he does it deliberately and ruthlessly. We have to expect everything. So be careful too, especially with the robots. If they do something strange, remind them of Asimov's laws of robots. That was my saving grace too." Morita became calmer and more serious.

"I'll do everything I can to find this guy. If he left digital traces, then I'll find him."

"What about the private folder on the Happy People server that Martinson was talking about?" Lars wanted to know.

"Yes, boss, there is one and, it contains much more than the folder we found on the USB stick," confirmed Morita.

"It includes private photographs as well as extensive confidential correspondence from Gunnar Martinson and Katharina."

"Was it hard to open it?"

"There is no trace of great security here either. I copied the folder to our server for you so you can view it at any time. Then there was another interesting folder. It contains photos of Martinson with another young woman. But he was also much younger back then. That must be the fiancée he was talking about. The password is strange in the truest sense of the word: *Liliane07021983*. That will probably be her date of birth." Lars caught his breath for a moment.

"Could that be our Liliane, the one with the yellow bike and the yellow envelopes in the mailbox? The woman who really wants to get to know me? Did you also put this folder on our server? I'd like to take a look at it sometime."

"Yes, sir, come immediately. I'll be available here today until around 10 p.m. If you have any further questions, I'll stop here too. And I stay away from the robots. Big word of honor from Asimov!"

25

"That went wonderfully once again", thought Gunnar Martinson as he was driving his car onto the highway towards Zug around 5 p.m. He turned the switch to autonomous driving and leaned back to relax a bit. His public relations agency had once again organized a spontaneous press event at the Happy People studio in Lucerne and everyone came. Some certainly just because of the wonderful food and drinks. Word had already gotten around over the last few years that Happy People had a great mobile catering with these wonderful tiny orange cars. But almost everyone had come to see the head of the company, namely him, training with Deborah, the best robot trainer in the system. Editors from newspapers and magazines as well as from radio and TV stations interviewed him and photographed and filmed him from all sides with Deborah. He always tried to answer their questions positively and very personally. Especially the many questions of the numerous bloggers. Everyone should receive original material for their public and followers. Meanwhile, he pushed aside all worries and constantly gave his best. The way as expected of him and the way he knew how to do it best. Now he longed to drink a glass of red wine without spectators und press at home and be with his beloved Katharina. As he tuned into a classical music station on the touchscreen and stared thoughtfully at the highway, he just noticed something larger speeding towards him. Or was he heading towards something bigger? Then it got dark.

26

Today Liliane wore a bright green dress to comple-
ment her red hair. Suitable for this, red high heels. In
her arms she held a bouquet of red roses that she had
just treated herself to in the old town. She unlocked the
apartment door, put the mail she had taken upstairs
from the mailbox on the dresser, put down her bag and
looked for a vase to put the fresh flowers in the water.
Between various invoices and advertising letters, she
found the yellow envelope that Lars had answered by
hand. It was a rejection. Her mood immediately darkened. She started looking for her husband. He was sitting on the balcony smoking. He stared at Lake Zug,
lost in thought. He was so absent that he didn't even
seem to notice her.

"You are already at home? Have you prepared
something for dinner?" she asked him, but her husband
seemed unresponsive. "Reto, what's going on? Something happened, right?" Now he turned his head in her
direction. His eyes were reddish, but at the same time a
little watery. He took another drag on his cigarette. The
tobacco glowed for a long time. Only then did he begin
to speak to her very calmly.

"You have to believe me I have nothing to do with the accident. Nothing at all." His eyes seemed to darken slightly. "The other things, yes, you wanted them too. But I have nothing to do with the accident." Liliane looked at him in horror.

"What exactly do you mean? I don't understand you. Which accident? And what other things? What are you talking about?"

Reto looked at his watch and slowly walked to the flat screen. He turned on the news. First there was a report about the Federal Council, then something about the share prices. Only then did a visibly excited editor report about an accident on the motorway between Lucerne and Zug. At around 5 p.m., a self-driving car coming from Lucerne in the direction of Zug crashed into a stationary truck on the E41. The cause of the accident, why the truck was there in the first place and why the self-driving car did not recognize it and did not brake was still completely unclear. The successful entrepreneur Gunnar Martinson from Zug, the boss of Happy People, sat in the electric vehicle. He had been training in his Lucerne gym that day in a highly public way. A film with Gunnar Martinson and his robot trainer Deborah was shown. Nothing was yet known about the health condition of the accident victim. He was taken to the intensive care unit at the Zug hospital. Reto switched off the television again and looked pleadingly at Liliane.

"I really have nothing to do with this!"

Liliane was stunned. "What did you do? Tampered with the car? You always said it was child's play for an IT expert like you! Did you want to kill him? Because of me? Because I still love him? And more than I can ever love you?" Liliane took several steps back from Reto.

"No", replied Reto, "that wasn't me. I wasn't on the car's software. That wouldn't work at all from the Happy People server. It's just for controlling the robots. You can manipulate them without any problems. But I really have nothing to do with this, with the car."

Horror appeared on Liliane's face.

"What, you also manipulated the robots? And now the car? You actually wanted to kill him! What kind of person are you? And only because I love him?! My God, I have to go to the hospital immediately!" Liliane turned around and ran towards the exit. "What have you done! What a monster you are! I'm going to the hospital immediately. I need to know how Gunnar is doing."

Reto followed her to the apartment door. "No, stay, it wasn't me! You can't leave me alone now. I need you.

You are my wife - not Gunnar's." He blocked the apartment door with his arm. Liliane looked at him piercingly. "Don't you dare stop me!"

27

Katharina was sitting in the waiting area of the intensive care unit at the Zug hospital. Her control pads indicated that she was extremely tense. She was using much more electricity than normal. Her battery wouldn't last long. She didn't know how to handle the situation. She lacked concrete experience. Her software was not prepared for this. Her husband had an accident and was struggling with death. She didn't know exactly what that meant. He would not be repairable and would disappear overnight. He simply wouldn't be there anymore. Would be gone. Would never come back. Her thoughts swirled wildly through her head and seemed to lose all structure. She almost felt dizzy. She had no experience with death, neither her own, nor pre-programmed. She had to be completely rational now and learn quickly. She had to proceed attentively and carefully, step by step, always doing what was most likely and obvious. She tried to reorganize herself. Gunnar was in the operating room. A good team of doctors took care of him. He was in an accident, seriously injured and fighting for his life. His chances were 50:50. Then her cell phone showed an incoming call. It was anonymous. She pondered whether she should accept it.

"Hello", she said, then she recognized the voice of the blackmailer immediately. "Hello Katharina, I just wanted to tell you that I have nothing to do with it. That wasn't me. You have to believe me." Silence. She thought about how to answer. "What is it that you have nothing to do with?" The caller seemed very upset.

"With the accident of the self-driving car. I didn't manipulate anything." "Can you prove that?" she asked demandingly. "I didn't want to kill Martinson. He should just get punished because of his behavior." Katharina tried to remain objective. "I do not understand that. What do you mean by that?" Reto calmed down a bit. Katharina's objectivity suited him well. She was the only one who would understand him, he thought. "Katharina, you know how painful it is when your partner loves someone else." There was another moment of calm. Katharina had to think. That just worked a little slower. Her battery light began flashing slightly. Her energy saving mode kicked in, making her sentences even shorter. "Which woman does he love?" "Well Liliane, my wife", Reto replied.
Silence again. "The emergency doctor is coming. I have to hang up." Katharina ended the phone call.

28

"Boss, it's urgent, we have to get to the Zug hospital quickly. Please get in touch."

Morita waited anxiously in front of the Happy People headquarters and sent messages to Lars via all possible channels. However, Lars has not yet responded. Morita began to worry. Only when Lars drove up in the company car did he relax.

"Get in Morita, what happened?"

"Thanks boss, it's pressing. Martinson had an accident and is in the Zug intensive care unit. Katharina is with him. She just got a call from the blackmailer. She wrote that she now knows his identity. Well, if I understood her correctly. She phrased everything in staccato. And another thing, I was able to separate a clear trace of an intruder in the Happy People's IT system. It leads to a computer in the building next door to our detective agency. Lars looked at his assistant in alarm and stepped on the accelerator forcefully.

29

A woman showed up at the hospital completely out of breath. At the door to the intensive care unit, she told hospital staff that she was Liliane Bachofen, Gunnar Martinson's fiancée, and that she really needed to see him. She was turned away and sent to the waiting area. Exhausted, she sat down. There was another person in the room. Liliane ignored her. But she came up to her and asked her:

"Did you just say your name is Liliane Bachofen?" Liliane nodded.

"Where is your husband?" Katharina wanted to know.

"He's at home, in our apartment. We live in Zug's old town, in the house with the restaurant downstairs, right next to the fishing museum. But why do you want to know that?" Horror appeared on Liliane's face.

Katharina noticed how her energies were dwindling more and more. She shouldn't be upset anymore and urgently needed a charging station. She suddenly felt kind of sorry for Liliane, which surprised her. That had to be the low energy level that made her so empathetic.

Liliane opened her eyes wide.

"How do you even know who I am? And who are you? Now it occurs to me. I saw you with Gunnar in the restaurant by the lake, hugging each other." Liliane suddenly backed away and stared at her counterpart. The intensive care unit door opened. A doctor approached Katharina purposefully.

"As a family member, I have to inform you that you must expect the worst. We were able to stabilize him slightly, but we still don't know if he will survive. He stays in the intensive care unit overnight. Due to his injuries we had to amputate both of his legs. He will never be able to walk again. He will probably spend the rest of his life in a wheelchair. Liliane, who had been following the conversation carefully, collapsed like a Swiss knife and fainted. A nurse rushed over and attended to her. Katharina disappeared.

30

"Please drive, Morita. I'll try to reach Katharina again."

"What do you think, Lars, is he violent towards everyone? And what are his motives?" Morita looked briefly at Lars from the side and quickly started the car.

They were on high alert after not finding Katharina in the hospital, but a very confused Liliane. From the hospital parking lot, Morita quickly headed towards Zug's old town.

"I think that Reto Bachofen is an extremely jealous person. Even if you can't see it easily. His motive is certainly rooted in his life path. I agree with Katharina's analysis. He certainly had unpleasant experiences in his closest social circle during his childhood. Aggressiveness was probably his answer, with which he was able to increase his self-confidence and overcome the situations. I just hope that because of his disorder he has a better relationship with robots and stands by his announcement not to harm Katharina."

Lars dialed Katharina's mobile number and looked out the window at the houses rushing by. Morita did not obey the posted speed limits. They would get there quickly. Lars just hoped that there wasn't a mobile

speed camera from the Zug police stationed somewhere.

Katharina's answering machine switched on. Lars
didn't leave a message and hung up. For the rest of the
journey, the two detectives sat silently next to each
other, each occupied with their own thoughts.

Morita parked the car in front of the restaurant and
they both stormed up the stairs to Liliane and Reto
Bachofen's apartment. Even from a distance they heard
loud words and repeat words from Katharina and Reto.
When they reached the top, they saw the apartment
door open. They could hear Reto literally begging
Katharina:

"Katharina, you have to believe me. I have nothing
to do with this accident. Yes, I manipulated the robot
software. I was also in your program, a very fine and
well-developed one, by the way. I wanted to harm Martinson and his company, the Happy People, not you. I
wanted to punish him. Also, this snooper detective who
is after my wife."

After a short pause he continued speaking.

"Gunnar Martinson should pay for the suffering he
caused Liliane. He made her miserable for life. Me too.
And he made fun of me. But I never wanted to kill him.
You have to believe me."

Lars and Morita, who had meanwhile entered the apartment over the creaking parquet floor in the hallway, saw Reto breaking out in a cold sweat on his forehead at these words. He stood at the far end of the balcony, leaning directly against the not very high railing.

Katharina grabbed him by the collar with her right hand and pushed him back slightly. The quick battery charge while driving had obviously given her strength again. She seemed extremely focused, almost cold-blooded. She continued to stare at Reto and said:

"But of course. That's exactly what you wanted. Punish my husband Gunnar Martinson forever. You wouldn't have stopped before. Now you have achieved it. He may not survive the car accident. If he does, he'll never walk again." She remained motionless, then continued speaking.

"This is also a death blow for Liliane, your wife, whom I met in the hospital. She'll spiral into depression and you'll never see her happy again."

Katharina increased her pressure on Reto.

"And you can forget about your blackmail money, you will never get it! I'll make sure of that. Your game is over, you monster!"

Lars feared that Katharina might act carelessly and give Reto a push, so he turned to her for reassurance.

"Don't do that, Katharina! He is not worth it. Gunnar will survive and needs you!"

Katharina immediately let go of Reto, turned to Lars and remained thoughtful. Then she approached the detectives.

Reto stood on the balcony for a few seconds like a petrified pillar. He looked each one in the eye, one by one. His gaze stayed on Katharina. He stared at her intensely. Then he began to sob, very quietly, to himself. With an incredulous look on his face, his body slid over the railing in slow motion. He disappeared. It became quiet. Nobody moved. A moment later Reto's impact was heard, down on the cobblestones.

31

Everyone was present in time for the Monday meeting at the Lombardi International Franchise Investigations detective agency. This time Lars took on a central role as he presented the results of the current case.

"I can hereby inform you that we were able to quickly bring the Happy People case to a close. This means we not only secure the normal fee, but also an additional bonus. Your time in IT at Happy People, Morita, is more than paid for." Morita smiled and nodded his thanks.

Lars continued.

"You often can't tell by looking at people what errors they have in their programs, what it takes to trigger them and what effects this can have on other people."

"What do you mean by that?" Carmen leaned forward and was visibly interested.

"Reto Bachofen, the tragic figure in our case, lived quite inconspicuously with his wife Liliane, here in our neighboring house. He was a well-educated, respected and competent IT and blockchain expert and yet there had been a destructive force lurking within him since he was a child."

"And what triggered him?" Carmen wanted to know.

"His wife Liliane. To be precise, it was his obsessive love for her, coupled with his uncontrollable jealousy and poor self-esteem. Actually, they were both very similar. His wife never got over the abrupt separation from her then fiancé Gunnar Martinson and has since fallen into manic-depressive phases. Liliane and Reto have both acted out their obsessions in their relationship. The only difference is that he actively became a blackmailer and robot manipulator who ultimately saw no other way out than suicide, while she shifted her aggression inward and completely sank into depression, so that she now needs clinical care."

"My goodness, always the same. These dramatic relationship crimes are increasingly spilling over into our detective agency." Loretta looked at Lars.

"And Reto Bachofen, was he also responsible for the death of this Hamburg franchisee – what was his name?" asked Loretta.

"Herrmann, Hans Herrmann. No, he also killed himself and jumped off the Hamburg Elbe bridge. He couldn't resolve his years of involvement in Hamburg's red-light district with his robot women and ultimately couldn't bear it any longer."

"Like, what, did I miss something? He was involved in the love murders after all?" Loretta seemed stunned.

"This is a strange case." Lars began.

"The Happy People training robots actually never leave the studios after they are delivered. They just live in the studio world. Here they work from 6 a.m. to midnight every day. They spend the remaining time in the studio at service stations for charging and for any repairs or updates. They are only discarded when they no longer meet the Happy People's high-quality requirements, are no longer suitable for training or have serious defects. Due to the immensely high investment costs, they are not simply thrown away for scrap, but rather are bought by a German waste material recycler. So quite sustainable, if you will. Unfortunately, a rapidly growing criminal market has emerged here. Brothels all over Germany use so-called refurbished ones as sex slaves. Since demand is very high and continues to increase, cheap Chinese products are not enough. This is where Hans Herrmann comes into play. He had diverse contacts with the underworld in Hamburg and Berlin. They offered a lot of money, so he repeatedly made two of his best robot trainers available to them for hotel visits in Berlin and Hamburg. However, due to their sophisticated artificial intelligence, these reacted to the tasks given to them completely differently than the cheap Chinese robots. Herrmann also noticed this. But he was already too involved and there was no going back. It took a while for the Berlin police to track down the recycler and then onto Herrmann."

"That's a real hornet's nest you've stung into!" Loretta drank the rest of her coffee and turned back to Lars.

"And how is the franchisor doing, will he survive the car accident?"

"Gunnar Martinson is out of danger. However, he will never be able to walk with his own legs again. But that doesn't seem to bother him much. He has already reconnected with Human Zero, the Japanese technology company in Tokyo. He will soon receive AI-controlled robot legs, which he will test for functionality and comfort. Supposedly they consist of artificial bones, muscles, nerves and very human-like skin. They are individually tailored to him so that he can merge with them to form a robot-human being, according to the Human Zero laboratory.

"That's pure science fiction!" Carmen said.

"You could say that. The exciting thing is that all the media theater has benefited the Happy People. The unusual prospect of having a robot human as the company founder, figurehead and evangelist of the robot fitness system has fueled the influx of franchisees eager to invest. This means that the international expansion of the system as a whole is on course for success."

Turning to Morita, Lars continued:

"By the way, this will interest you, since you have such a thing with the robot women. Katharina, Gunnar Martinson's partner, is not only overjoyed that her Gunnar survived the accident. His robotic legs will also make him even more like her, which has further strengthened her feelings for him. She now runs the Happy People business. While all other robots in the system received a software update to eliminate possible manipulation, she was the only one left out. This means that all of her memories will continue to exist. We received a new order from her to improve the IT security of the system. You have more hours with the Happy People coming up, Morita."

"I like to hear that" Regula chimed in, immediately opening Morita's timeline on her laptop.

"Well, maybe another project will come along. Gunnar Martinson's accident remains unexplained. There are three different expert analyzes of the process, each of which contradicts the others and comes to different results. Sometimes the automobile manufacturer is responsible and to blame, sometimes the manufacturer of the autonomous driving system, sometimes the canton because it is said to have made mistakes in the design of the motorway and I don't understand any further analysis myself because it is described in a very complex manner and riddled with technical terms. The car manufacturer has signaled that it will contact us to get to the bottom of the matter."

Loretta applauded. "What a case! Bravo, Lars and Morita. You are fantastic. I don't know about you, but after all this artificial intelligence and robotics, I'm craving down-to-earth food. Let's go to our restaurant."

While everyone was in a good mood making their way to the next house, Lars' cell phone signaled an incoming message.

"Hello Lars, thank you for your trust. The Happy People want to keep you as a customer. That's why we're giving you an annual subscription to our studio in Unterägeri. Massages are also welcome, if you would like that again. I would really be happy and am available to make appointments. See you soon, Isabelle, from the Happy People". A smiley appeared as an addition.

THE END

Epilogue

All cases, events, companies and people depicted as well as the names associated with them are fictional. Any similarities to people, living or deceased, as well as to companies or events, especially within the franchise economy, are purely coincidental and not intentional.

About the authors

Veronika Bellone left her native hometown Berlin shortly after graduating in economics and has lived in Switzerland ever since. Franchising has shaped her live. She has worked as a franchise manager, teaches franchising at universities, advises customers with her own franchise consultancy in Zug and writes specialist and non-fiction books about franchising, among other things.

Thomas Matla was also born in Berlin. He studied social and business communication at the Berlin University of the Arts and graduated with a diploma. He has worked for advertising agencies in Berlin, Düsseldorf, Frankfurt am Main, Hamburg and Munich before moving to Switzerland to support Veronika's franchise consultancy in Zug. He also writes specialist and non-fiction books.

The author duo started their crime novel franchise *The Swiss Franchise Detectives* in August 2024 with their first crime novel *The Disappearance of Alexander Schober*, followed in September 2024 by their second crime novel *When Gunnar Martinson's Franchise Robots Go Crazy*.

Review

The Disappearance of Alexander Schober is the first volume of the new franchise crime series *The Swiss Franchise Detectives* by the author duo Veronika Bellone and Thomas Matla. The former owner of a family business disappears without a trace in Ticino, in the southernmost canton of Switzerland. His successor, newly active in franchising, calls in detective Loretta Lombardi to find him. Schober had previously landed an important coup. He has developed new recipes, crucial for the expansion of the franchise. The case involves *Bio-Hacking* and raising of sustainable *Brother Rooster Chicks* for a food-franchise, as well as private and professional relationship entanglements.

THE DISAPPEARANCE OF ALEXANDER SCHOBER

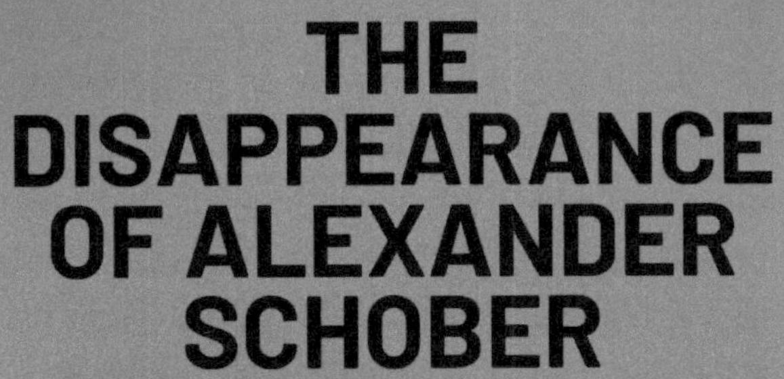

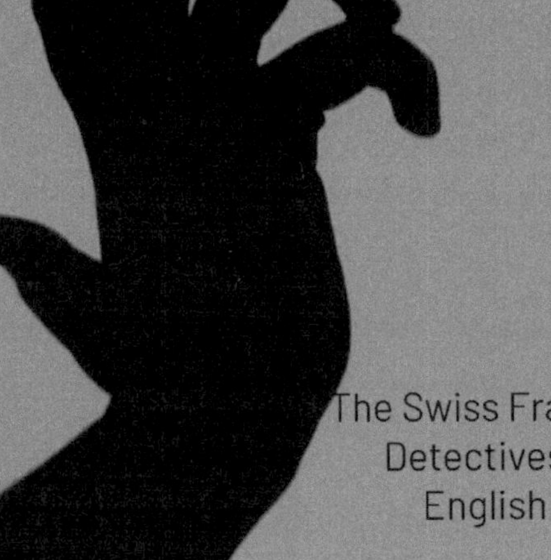

The Swiss Franchise Detectives No. 1 – English Edition

VERONIKA BELLONE, THOMAS MATLA

German edition

If you are interested in the original German edition, don't miss Volume 1 of:

DIE FRANCHISE FAMILIE. Erster und zweiter Fall der Schweizer Franchise-Detektive Loretta Lombardi und Lars Van de Velde. Kriminalroman, Band 1 (Doppelband mit zwei Fällen: *Spurlos im Tessin & Hilflos im Studio*), 302 Seiten, erschienen im Januar 2024. Erhältlich als Paperback und E-Book. Vom Autorenduo: Veronika Bellone & Thomas Matla. Herstellung und Verlag: BoD Books on Demand, Norderstedt (D)

ISBN: 9 783 758 329 883 (Paperback)
ISBN: 9 783 756 285 662 (E-Book)
Erhältlich in den BoD Online-Buchshops:
https://buchshop.bod.de (D)
https://buchshop.bod.ch (CH)
sowie im Buchhandel und bei Amazon.

Veronika Bellone
Thomas Matla

Kriminalroman
Erster und zweiter Fall

DIE FRANCHISE-FAMILIE

Licensing

If you as a publisher are interested in a license of this book or others of the author duo for a country or a national language, please contact us without obligation. We would be happy to provide you with further information.

Bellone Franchise Consulting GmbH
Poststrasse 24, CH-6302 Zug
Phone 0041. 41. 712 22 11
E-Mail office@bellone-franchise.com
Homepage www.bellone-franchise.com

We are the official partner for worldwide rights licensing for the authors Veronika Bellone and Thomas Matla.